Dovetail

Dovetail

Jeremy
Hughes

ALCEMI

In Memory of
Russell Roofe and Bob Stanton

First impression: 2011

© Jeremy Hughes, 2011

Published with the financial support of the Welsh Books Council

Editor: Gwen Davies
Cover design: Matthew Tyson

ISBN: 978-0-9560125-3-1

Printed on acid-free and partly-recycled paper.
Published by Alcemi and printed and bound in Wales by
Y Lolfa Cyf., Talybont, Ceredigion SY24 5HE
e-mail ylolfa@ylolfa.com
website www.alcemi.eu
tel 01970 832 304
fax 01970 832 782

Man is a tool-using Animal.
Nowhere do you find him without tools;
Without tools he is nothing,
With tools he is all.

Thomas Carlyle

You must either make a tool of the creature, or a man of him.
You cannot make both.

John Ruskin

Chapter One

Strange that I knew I would use it to kill. Stranger that I knew I would use it to kill them. Strangest that I knew this at the age of fifteen.

But I did. I know now that people think of fifteen-year olds as too young to experience such prescience, but I didn't think it odd that those who were making my life hell would eventually pay for their cruelty in moments of such sublime calculation, moments of considered poise.

That they might mature beyond their adolescent silliness into people of stature – though I'm not sure what I mean by that – never entered into it. It didn't matter. Their cruelty was such that I resolved it deserved punishment at some point I had yet to determine.

They might think it unbelievable but before their lungs had manufactured their last breaths they would appreciate (it's good to have an audience) the fantastic manner of their deaths. No protracted hospital-bed demise for them. Rather a death beautifully conceived, carefully prepared and expertly executed. It wasn't lost on me that I had gone to so much expense, learning and privation for their sakes. I had made a thing of beauty and I had made it for them. They were all going to die with a grace greater than they could have ever understood. They should be grateful.

The Butt Joint is the simplest. It is merely one member meeting another with no form of 'marriage' or interlocking parts cut in each member. It is not a strong joint and is made stronger by reinforcing it in some way. Butt Joints are used for light frames or small boxes. They can be square-cut or mitred (when two members meet, each cut to 45 degrees) and are usually nailed for strength.

Bull. Because of his large penis. *Twp.*[1] Walked like an orangutan, long and loose-armed. He offered me a swig from his coke can one day.

---

[1]   Welsh, meaning stupid. Pronounced: w as the vowel in *put*

"There's a bit in the bottom," he said. I took the warmth of the can as the heat from his hand and tipped my head right back. I didn't recognise the taste. He'd urinated in it.

Bull was lemon.

I realised my vocation in life on the third of July, 1978. I understood that it would take a long time but didn't realise that it would be eighteen years later when I would finally fulfil my calling. I had spilled my pot of water in the Art room and had to mop the floor. With the heat beating against the window like a bee, I was content to leave late and, because there would be no one at home, I cut across the fields to the canal instead of taking the direct route along the road.

Dog. Because he was always picking up dog-ends and saving them for later. Wiry. Bandy. Not bad on his own but he could change at the blink of an eye. Would do anything Napper egged him on to do. I thought of him as Deputy, as in Deputy Dawg, but never said it.

The only time I saw him on his own was with an air rifle along the canal. He shot a *Chloris chloris*[2] out of the top of a *Fagus sylvatica*[3] and it plunged into the water, where it flapped and flapped, frantically trying not to drown, until he shot it again and again until it stopped.

Dog was lime but occasionally orange.

The claw hammer is probably the most versatile tool in the craftsman's box. It is available in different weights and though it would be ideal to have each of them, if you have a tight budget, then you should purchase the heaviest, which is 24 ounces. Its weight does take some getting used to but it drives in nails with less effort than lighter hammers. It is also essential for taking out mis-hit nails or de-nailing timber. These are not the only uses, however. It can be used for marrying pieces or even demolition. It is surprising how versatile and 'handy' it is, and many craftsmen wear them in a belt clip.

There are many manufacturers but you cannot beat Estwing for balance or looks. A craftsman interested in creating objects of beauty must surely care, too,

[2] Greenfinch
[3] European beech

about the aesthetics of his tools. The Estwing hammer has a handle made up of thin strips of leather wound tightly around the shaft, which is then sealed.

There were two fields, the path running down the hedge of one and diagonally across the other to the metal gate. Then it took you through trees tight on either side to the stone bridge over the canal to the towpath. I was surprised at the gate.

Ev. Evans. Prop. Just because of his size and the fact that other kids bounced off him when he ran at them. If he wore a hat, his hair would have looked like a scarecrow. Lumbering. Laughed like a moron. Once he sat a History exam, wrote his name on the top of the paper, read the questions, then put his pen down. I could feel him looking at me as I filled page after page about the Spinning Jenny[4] and the Seed Drill.[5] He shouted after me on the way home. "Wanker!"
   Ev was orange.

Ripsaws are the largest of the handsaws, having five points per inch (5 PPI) and approximately two feet two inches long. It is a specialised tool for cutting solid timber down the grain. These take some getting used to because of their size and to make a straight cut takes a good deal of practice.

   Crosscut saws are a similar size but have 6 to 8 PPI and are very good for cutting planks to length.

   Panel saws are shorter (approximately one foot nine inches) and have 10 to 12 PPI. The number of teeth makes them ideal for man-made boards as well as general crosscutting.

I didn't know of the timber I would use until I started work on the design. When I came to it, my immediate inclination was *quercus robur,*[6] but I soon discounted that as a silly cliché. Very silly. It was fine in Nelson's ships but such dense and quite vulgar grain wouldn't express

---

[4]   Invented in 1764 by James Hargreaves (1720–1778), a weaver and carpenter
[5]   Invented in 1701 by Jethro Tull (1674–1741), agriculturist
[6]   European oak. Can be called English or French, depending on its origin. Leaves distinct blue dye on the hands when worked

the feminine finesse I had in mind. *Diospyros ebenum*,[7] however, soon presented itself as a magnificent choice for the intricate details that would be essential for my happiness.

From the outset, though, I decided that I would use solid timber throughout. There would be no veneers and the more I refined the design the greater my choice of timbers became. She would be a jewel of hardwood exotica.

Napper aka Matthew Rand. Blonde. A leader. Everything he wanted. Father who turned up for everything and who kitted him out in all the best sports gear. Cricket, for example: whites, pads, gloves, box, bat. Wickets even. A thump or kick was his way of saying hello, though he was never actually saying "Hello". It was his way of letting you know where you were. And where you were was way below him in the pecking order. And that's where you were going to stay.

What I never understood was why he was universally adored by girls. They shivered when he was near. I trembled. On the inside, that is, tensed for the dig in the ribs, trip in the dinner queue, the slam into a corridor wall.

Napper was strawberry.

Halving Joints are cut in members of equal dimensions and half the thickness is cut from each. They are straightforward to cut and used where one member crosses another. They can be cut by machine or by handsaw and chisel. There is nothing more satisfying than cutting joints by hand. The most obvious example of a halving joint is in the crossed members of the crucifix.

So surprised, I can remember exactly what I was thinking about when they took me: tench. The first I'd ever caught. It had been a Sunday and I was looking out of my bedroom window over the roofs of the houses opposite, the mountain on the other side of the valley lost in low cloud. It had been raining heavily and my mother (Mam) wouldn't let me go out until it eased.

---

[7]   Ebony. Commonly used in the manufacture of musical instruments

I'd been poring over *The Angling Times*, an issue I'd had so long it was falling apart, with photographs of men or boys – never women – holding specimen fish or displaying large catches on grass in front of them. My rod – all six feet of it – was already tackled up. All I had to do was put the worm on the hook and cast.

I climbed over the gate and started to walk along the path to the bridge when my name was called from behind. I turned to see Ev with Bull.

"All right," I said.

"*We're* all right."

I carried on towards the bridge, thinking I'd be able to speed up as soon as I got to the towpath. But Napper and Dog were there.

The first time I saw *Dalbergia nigra*[8] was the box in which my grandfather (Bampa) kept his pocket watch. I was mesmerised by the rich, high figure of its grain. It was inlaid with mother of pearl and there was a flower-shaped escutcheon in the middle of the lid. When my grandfather died, my grandmother (Nan) said I could have something which had belonged to him. I asked for the box. I keep precious things in it.

When the rain gave up, I stuffed my gear – I didn't even have a tackle box – into my parka pockets and went down the canal. I had a favourite spot, an overhanging sycamore which, when it was sunny, created a dark and mysterious shade where fish *must* be. Up to that point I had only caught perch and roach, and not many of them. All small.

My first cast went straight into the overhanging branches and the line snapped as soon as I tried to pull it back. Losing the hook and lead shot was no problem, really, but the float, dangling bright and red-tipped against the sycamore leaves, hurt: it was half a week's pocket money. Great start, I thought.

It had started raining again, heavily, and it was tricky tying a new hook on the line without it puncturing my index finger or thumb, which, though it wouldn't have been life threatening, meant I would have had to go straight home and probably to hospital because of the

[8] Brazilian Rosewood

barb. Hooks are barbless now.

The float I used was an old quill. It was all I had left. The paint had worn off the tip so that it was just going to be its peculiar ivory whiteness against the green water.

Already the rain was penetrating the seams of the parka across my shoulders, and so hard it was difficult to tell if it were falling onto the water or shooting up from it. But where the sycamore drooped, the water was more or less still.

The next cast was going straight into the branches again and I flicked it back as soon as I realised, the whole rig stinging past my face into the long grass behind. I composed myself before I cast again. This time the float had hardly settled in the water when it shot straight under.

A good set of bevel-edge chisels is essential. They are used for removing waste from joints and the smaller chisels are used for shaping and trimming. The most useful is the one-inch (25 mm), which is often used for removing glue from the joints of a project when it is being clamped up. As with any edged tool, it must be used only when sharp. The adage that a blunt tool is a dangerous tool must be respected. A craftsman whose tools are not maintained to the highest order is not a craftsman.

Craftsmen use a variety of 'tests' to check the sharpness of a chisel (or a plane iron, for that matter). Some run it along the arris of a piece of timber, some slice into the skin on the tip of a finger so that a sliver is raised (not recommended for beginners), some present the edge to the hairs on the back of a hand.

It is amazing how harshly modern chisels can be treated. The composite handles have a strength which permits great strike forces to be received from mallets or hammers.

As soon as I struck into the bite, I realised that it was a big fish. Big by my standards, that is. It pulled the line straight to the opposite bank and in the short time it took me to land, I believed it would be much larger than it turned out to be. Still, it was by far the most impressive fish I had ever caught. I placed it gently on the thick grass to admire it and could hardly get my hand around its girth to remove the hook from its thick lip. There was such evenness to its green that I have not seen a jewel so intense since. Although it must have been only a pound in weight, it made all the other fish I had caught up to that point insignificant, merely a preparation for this magical moment. I put it back in the water.

"We've been waiting for you," Napper said.

"Waiting?" The tench was suspended just below the surface of the water, its pectoral fins clearly visible like gently wafting fans.

"That's what he said," Dog chipped in. "That's what he said."

"You're a right little fucker, you," said Napper, looking up at me. Oh why couldn't I just shrug him off?

I collapsed to the ground when Bull thrust his knees into the backs of mine and when I hit the deck he kicked me. Then they all kicked me.

It *was* happening. Not knowing what was coming next was like watching my float in the water, expecting something to happen but not knowing what or when.

Chapter Two

I knew I'd be back when I had acquired the skills I needed. I would organise reunions which, as far as I knew, had never taken place around here. There was no need for them. Everyone knew where everyone else was; they saw each other in the village or in the pubs weekly if not daily.

I was the one who had gone.

Not from where the teenage new Kingdom Pharoah was buried in a coffin of gold three thousand three hundred years ago, nor where directors shouted *Action!* at dusty cowboys or cavalry or Navajo extras as they chased or fought or brooded close up into the eye of the camera, the distant sandstone skyscrapers foretelling modern American architecture, but where, as a child, I saw miners going down and coming up, white and black, before the pits were closed, flattened and landscaped, the industrial waste grounds planted with a solitary coal truck or wheel of the head-gear, paltry memorials for the boys, men, canaries and ponies who worked, coughed, spewed and died under the sopping, sodden, sodding weight of the World.

That first moment with Jesús, I knew I'd learn what I needed to learn. I stood in the open doorway of the house[9] I'd seen from the road, with a bag in each hand but, as I'd been in strong sunlight, I could not see into the darkness of the room. I called out but received no reply. Then he appeared, wearing a leather apron and carrying a piece of wood.

"*Hola*," I said, "*Busco* Jesús-María Barriales."

He looked me up and down, then motioned for me to follow him.

He led me through the room to another door, flicked on a light and pointed me to a low plinth in the middle of the floor. He took my bags and walked around me slowly, looking intensely the whole time. But it's what happened next that convinced me. He flicked another switch and a flash of light crunched my pupils into diamonds.

[9]   Casa Arbol

I was lit from all sides by spots so powerful that it felt as though they were penetrating my skin to the bones. I held up my hand for shade and could just discern him walking around me. One moment his face was so close to mine it was as if he were an ophthalmologist carrying out an examination, the next he took my hands and turned them over in his hands, spreading the fingers, squeezing them individually, digging his thumb and forefinger into the flap of skin which joined my thumbs to the forefingers. My arms next. Feeling them from the shoulder down to the wrist, ending with them extended while he sighted along them, first from the shoulder to the fingertips, then from the fingertips to the shoulder.

It is a general truth that there is a specific tool for a specific purpose. This is obviously true of bench planes. The largest of these is a try (or jointer) plane, typically two feet long and used for making straight edges, for example, for the butt-jointed planks of a table top. The two main types of bench plane are the jack plane and the smoothing plane. Jack planes are used to plane surfaces square and flat. Smoothing planes are shorter and used more for finishing. Although it is still possible to purchase wooden planes, most planes today are of cast metal. Some of these planes have grooved soles which reduces the friction with the timber. This is especially helpful when working with resinous timbers.

Block planes are small and used one-handed (though there is a knurled brass knob on the toe on which to exert pressure with your free hand). The irons are set low[10] in order to make very fine cuts. It is for this reason that they are ideal for trimming end grain.

The lights went out and I was left on the plinth. My bags came into focus but Jesús was gone. I stepped off the plinth and heard noises off to the right, coming from another room. Jesús was making coffee when I entered. He put two beautiful turquoise cups on the table (which I was surprised to see was roughly hewn and nailed together), and pulled out a chair for me to sit.

"Okay," he said. "We'll see how we get on."

I was taken aback. "You speak English."

---

[10] 20 degrees, though there are some in which the blade is set as low as 12 degrees

"I *am* English. Just prefer the name Jesús. He was a better man than James Raymond, late of the parish of, well…"

"I just thought." I didn't know what I thought.

He poured coffee into both of the cups.

"You have pretty hands," he said.

"Oh. Thank you."

"It's not a compliment," he said, "there's no strength in them. But all's not lost. They're a good shape, and your arms are true."

"Right."

He pushed the coffee towards me. "So…"

I nodded. I looked at the table.

"It was here when I arrived," he said, by way of explanation. "It's honest."

I was to hear him describe pieces as being honest many times after that.

Ochroma lagopus[11] **is a very odd timber. Most people immediately think it is a softwood because it is so incredibly light. It is extremely soft, also, which creates a false sense of security. It has to be treated very gently in order that any cuts – whether from saws or edge tools – do not go too deep. To attain a good finish takes a great deal of patience. It has traditionally been used for making model aeroplanes.**

It wasn't really a room, but a large, high-ceilinged building in which there were two full-sized benches and tools stored on cupboard shelves and bespoke racks. My knowledge of tools was poor but I longed to hold them and use them, each in its way a marvel. Each was imbued with a reason for being. I envied them. I envied them when Jesús used them to fulfil their function and was able to translate his designs from two dimensions to three. I wanted the certainty of those tools, to have my reason for being made real. All I had, then, was an urge to create something beautiful and real and functional, but I had much to learn if this were to be achieved.

"Everything is done by hand," Jesús said, "everything. That's why

---

[11] Balsa

15

it all costs so much more. A great deal more. You can't make anything unless you have known the wood intimately. Machines come between the wood and the maker."

My first lesson was how to keep the workshop clean.

The timber store was enormous, full of species I had never seen and names I had never heard. They were arranged in colour from light to dark, from *Dyera costulata*[12] to *Dalbergia cearensis*,[13] *Tilia americana*[14] to *Guibourtia demeusei*.[15] This would be the palette with which I would work. I would woo my darling into life in order that she may love the men who deserved to be loved so well. In a manner I determined.

You will need a variety of measuring and marking-out tools. The traditional folding rule is made of boxwood (some antique rules are made of ivory) and most useful if it has inches on one face and millimetres on the other. Some rules have a bevel-edge to enable accurate marking, essential for high-class work where precision is paramount.

Rules are usually one metre but they can also be found in mini sizes suitable for a leg or apron pocket.

For laying-out rods, twelve, twenty-four and thirty-six-inch metal engineering rules are necessary.

It was a warm September day in Paris when I first came across Jesús's work. I'd been to the Musée de la Revolution to see the guillotine and took lunch in the Gallerie Nouveau. There it was.

Years later, when I'd been with Jesús long enough to know when was a good time to ask him if I could see his designs, I saw it again in all its stages of development, from the first tentative sketches (none the less extraordinary for that) to the final scale drawings, the timbers and fittings labelled in his beautiful hand. Then there were the photographs – one of them in situ where I'd seen it – and finally, the mock-up in balsa.

"It's just as I remember it," I said.

---

12 Jelutong
13 Kingwood
14 Basswood
15 Bubinga

"No it isn't, but... it's...."

I had learned not to pursue something he had left in mid-air. He had a habit of closing his eyes and shaking his head, as if to say, let it go.

It looked like a cabinet but, of course, that would have been too easy. Anyone can make a cupboard. But only Jesús, as far as I knew then, could have made this.

The Mortise and Tenon joint is versatile, being used in many joinery and cabinet-making applications, from internal doors to fine furniture. As with most joints today, the modern workshop can prepare them using specialist machinery. But it is worth learning how to cut a mortise and tenon joint by hand in order to appreciate its structure. Each member – the mortise and tenon – must be cut absolutely square if the joint is to be strong. As mortise chisels are normally used in the workshop environment, they are struck with a mallet[16] rather than a hammer.

A through mortise and tenon joint can be made particularly attractive by using wedges of a contrasting timber species, making a feature of the joint. It is worth remembering that customers' tastes vary considerably and it may be necessary to 'guide' them to accepting a design which is not overloaded with such features. Good design is a case of 'less is more'. Quality makes itself heard through 'quiet' craftsmanship.

A very *nice* cabinet, I'll admit, in which to display a respectable home's cut-glass and decanters. An astute observer might have noticed that the depth of the shelves and the mirrored back didn't actually go as deep as the overall dimensions of the piece suggested. Behind the mirror was a high-security metal cabinet, in this case, for guns. The lower cupboard stored ammunition.

"Any piece – no matter what it is – must surprise in some way," Jesús said. "This is a crude surprise, but what the customer wanted. I did my best with the brief."

---

[16] Made of *Fagus sylvatica* (European beech) or *Lignum vitae* (greenheart)

"But not every piece can be surprising," I said.

"No, no, no. Not surprise in that sense. Surprise in its aesthetic, its proportions, its timbers, its design, its craftsmanship."

I wanted nothing more, at that instant, than to be a craftsman, to be as good as Jesús.

Try squares are essential for checking the accuracy of ninety-degree corners and marking right angles from one face to another. The favourite Try square of most craftsmen has a rosewood stock and a brass edge. The blade is held with diamond-shaped rivets to ensure that it will be able to sustain being knocked in the workshop. A twelve-inch square is suitable for most purposes but smaller tools will also be of benefit. Although the rosewood and brass square is aesthetically pleasing, it must be conceded that a tool with a cast iron stock will be more accurate because it is far less likely to be affected by its immediate climate.

The guillotine was stunning. The perfect machine for killing. Its very essence for being was utterly simple and it fulfilled this with clinical precision. But it lacked any kind of other-being, not engaging the recipients of its grace on any kind of meaningful level. And that 'grace' was mercy, yet what I wanted was to create something that was grace-full. Not merciful.

I started to design her after I had been with Jesús for five years. I had prevented myself from even contemplating the undertaking until I had the skills I deemed necessary and appropriate. I could have begun the design as soon as I arrived but would have produced something ugly and impractical. She had to be perfect and perfection would take experience, foresight and application.

I was taking coffee by the harbour in the city, listening to the jazz for which the Café del Mar was known locally, when I realised that I could begin. A yacht passed slowly, a stunning creature completely made of timber rather than the harsh white-hulled hulks of modernity. Every plank was integral to the yacht's purpose. It encapsulated everything my darling had to be. Each of her components had to be contributing to her being. So that's where she was conceived, on the café's menu, with a pencil borrowed from Gregorio who was waiting tables, all empty bar mine, ranged neatly towards the doors open to the harbour, the jazz almost imperceptible to my ears as I began the design which was to be refined and refined for years.

It wasn't until I had been with Jesús for several months that I learned the story of San Sebastian. Jesús insisted that my attendance at church was intrinsic to my apprenticeship. The interminable length of the mass, the queues for the confession boxes and the orchestra were to become greatly comforting.

Chapter Three

Napper, Ev, Dog and Bull surrounded me. I was bruised and my mind was running down corridors that didn't actually lead anywhere but ended in darkness.

Napper had a firm idea. Ev, Bull and Dog would carry it out. First, scare me. They were experts. They picked me up and dangled me off the parapet of the bridge above the water, letting me slide through their hands, gradually, until my trousers only were held, my weight (what there was of it) pulling hard on my belt which cut into me.

I was screaming and they were laughing. It felt like free-fall when they dropped me. I crumpled into the surface, the rank water infiltrating every pore. I dragged myself onto the bank, my school uniform feeling like wet cement. But I was relieved that it was over, that now they had had their fun, I could make my way home and avoid them as best I could the next day. I wished, intensely, that I had an older brother, or better, five older brothers who could have beaten them to a pulp. But it was just me, five feet eleven inches of skin and bone.

In my mind I was calling them every taboo word[17] I could think of, shouting them over and over in a tirade of incomprehensible vitriol. But, in that moment I fought back the tears and said absolutely nothing. My silence would buy me my freedom. They were laughing.

The design process is essential to the conception of any piece that is to be produced, therefore the following equipment must be regarded as necessary to the craftsman's toolkit: drawing board (with sliding parallel guide), set squares, compass, French curves, protractors, circle templates, scale rules, dividers.

When designing a piece, first impressions are usually sketched. These sketches are then transferred to a drawing board for scale drawing. It is important that the piece is

---

[17] I cannot bring myself even to write these words down

described in front, side and plan elevations. It may be necessary to draw specific features full-size because of their perceived difficulty and/or for clarity. Drawn sections show the piece's internal structures. Scale drawings are usually 1:4 when using the imperial system of measurement. It is good practice to make the drawings on tracing paper so that future drawings may be overlaid as the design develops. Scale drawings enable a model to be made out of balsa to examine the project in three dimensions. If necessary, a model can be made from the materials in which the project is to be realised. A full-size mock-up can be made from cheaper materials and scraps in the workshop. This can help to ensure that a project is structurally viable and proportionally balanced.

There are three specialist tools for making hand-cut dovetails: a dovetail template, a dovetail saw and a dovetail chisel.

A dovetail template looks like a brass butterfly with disproportionate 'wings'. These are tails, one for marking dovetails in softwood with a ratio of 1:6, the other for marking dovetails in hardwood with a ratio of 1:8.

The dovetail saw is a smaller version of the tenon saw. It is a backsaw, that is, it has a brass strip on the top edge of the blade. The weight this provides allows the cut to be made without the craftsman having to 'force' it. It also ensures that the blade is kept straight. Because of the nature of the dovetail joint, it has fine teeth, bearing between 16 and 22 PPI for cutting finely in hardwood.

The dovetail chisel is actually a Japanese chisel called a Shinogi-nomi. Its section is triangular and is ideal for removing the waste from the pins and tails of dovetail joints. They come in sizes between one-eighth to half-inch.

Bull picked me up in a bear-hug and I couldn't believe it.

"No!" I shouted. It merely fuelled their laughter. "I've had enough."

Their laughter continued. Still, I didn't struggle. In my reckoning it would make matters worse, even though at this stage I didn't know what was to come. But were I to fight I would have been hurt more.

They tied me to a *Quercus robur* with the belt from my trousers as if I were hugging the trunk. Then they pulled down my trousers and underpants and lifted my shirt over my head. No one had ever been tied to anything as far as I knew. The usual punishment was 'the line', which involved the victim running through two lines of people facing each other. When the first pair was reached it was a signal for the parallel lines to begin kicking. There was no way the end of the line could be reached before falling to the ground and then the lines encircled to kick indiscriminately. If you wouldn't run the line you had 'the corner' instead, which was merely being shoved in a corner and being kicked. Hobson's choice.

Above my head was a hole with wasps in the air around it. Napper pronounced wasp to rhyme with asp so that, to me, it sounded so much more sinister. I needn't have worried about them.

Napper came to my side. "Like it?" He showed me a sheath knife. "Birthday. Haven't used it yet."

I wanted to close my eyes.

He walked away and returned with a sycamore branch, stripping leaves as he spoke. "It's a bit green. Have to sort out the tip. Don't want to hurt anyone, do I?"

They all laughed.

"Got a pen?" Ev asked.

"Fuck do you want a pen for?" Napper said, taking a biro from his pocket. I felt it digging into my back. "Didn't know you were such an artist."

They were standing behind me laughing. In between the laughter I could hear the new knife stripping the branch. Strip. Strip. Strip. Silence and a sense of drawn breath. Then something winded me. Napper's branch appeared on the ground to my left, a few leaves left at the end like crude fletching, its tip cut flat so that it had butted my back.

"Shot!" said Bull.

"You're gonna be the next Leighton Rees,"[18] said Ev.

"Give it me," said Bull.

"Get your own, you fucker," Napper said.

[18] Professional Darts Player from Ynys–y–bŵl, south Wales

There was a flurry of activity then as each of them broke off branches. They took it in turns. Each punch was a surprise. Even with my whole body tensed, I couldn't prepare for the shock of each blow. Some hit me between my ribs, winding me, some hit me in the soft tissue over my kidneys, buckling my legs, some hit me on the scapulas with a crack that reverberated right through my skeleton. A couple hit me in the head and made me feel nauseous. Ev drew on my buttocks, then.

"Out the way, out the way!" Dog shouted, and before Ev could get clear I was hit three times quickly as Dog, Bull and Napper flung their sticks. Then there was a great deal of rustling and a long, long, long, long, long pause mixed with the knife fashioning the sycamore, before the blow which made them stop.

"Bullseye!" Napper shouted.

I felt something beyond comprehension. I realised, later, this must have been pain. The belt went loose. I felt sticky. They ran. I passed out.

Chapter Four

I watched everything he did for a long time. The way he held the tools, the way he stood, the way he looked at things. My first exercise alone was to cut a piece of *Prunus serotina*[19] into a twelve-inch square. It may sound easy but it took me a long time. I had to use a rule, try square, pencil, marking knife, panel saw, jack plane and block plane. When I had completed the task, Jesús examined it minutely with a try square and a rule:

- the face wasn't flat
- the face edges weren't all square
- the end-grain was uneven
- one end-grain corner fell away
- the dimensions were inaccurate.

Start again.

I was happy for my efforts to be criticised in such detail. I knew that I was with a master, someone who wouldn't settle for anything other than perfection. On the rare occasion that Jesús made an error, he would never try to rectify it or 'make good', but insisted on starting again. Even though this would take time – however considerable an amount – it ensured that whatever left the workshop was superb. It took me eleven attempts to get the square completed to Jesús's satisfaction, and when I had, I felt that I had achieved something astonishing.

I always returned to that square whenever I was considering letting something 'go', when I knew, deep down, it wasn't good enough. Whatever I did *had* to be right.

The church of San Pedro was in the centre of the city and my memory always tells me that when I entered the sky was grey and when I emerged the sky was blue. There were always gypsies or cripples[20] begging outside the doors and the first time I attended mass I was

---

[19] American Cherry
[20] That's what the locals called them

happy to give them the pesetas from my pockets. Jesús told me later not to bother. They were there every day, not just Saturdays when we attended. It was their living. No money from anywhere else. Whole families begged, he said, rotating outside the different churches in the city. Even the grey sky couldn't prepare me for the darkness inside. The church was already full. The only time I had seen a congregation of this size was at the school carol concerts at Ebenezer Chapel, but this was a Saturday morning.

"You sit there," Jesús said, pointing into the darkness on the left, while he took a seat close to the front.

From where I sat, I looked towards the priest in the subdued light, the congregation standing and sitting, standing and sitting, repeating his words or answering ritually. Everything was strange to me. Catholics were a rare species in the Valleys. I'd only ever seen a confession box in films but knew that whatever was disclosed to a priest would never be shared.[21] There was something deeply attractive about that. But what were these people – adults and children alike – saying to the priest in that confined space?

There were actually four confession boxes, exaggeratedly gothic in style, and two of them were busy receiving sinners who had transgressed from the holy doctrine, craving the neighbour's wife or husband, or leaving cafés without paying – albeit unintentionally – and who couldn't bring themselves to return. I wondered what a priest would say to me if I told him I was in Spain because I'd been tied to a tree at the age of fifteen by four boys who I was going to find again and kill. Would it make any difference if I said that they were going to die *beautifully*?

There are three main patterns for screwdrivers: slot-head, Phillips and Pozidriv. They come in many sizes and handle designs. The most important point is that the tip of the driver must fit the screw which is to be driven. Generally speaking, a screwdriver with a large handle fits the hand and facilitates good

---

[21] Montgomery Clift in *I Confess* (1953) plays a priest, Fr. Michael William Logan, who hears the confession of a murderer but will not share the confessional with the police

control. Cabinet screwdrivers are still favoured by cabinet makers for this reason. Fluted handles are plastic and the grip is less satisfactory.

Spiral ratchet screwdrivers are helpful when fixing numerous screws. Pressure on the handle is converted along grooves on its shaft into rotation at its tip. The shaft is spring-loaded and 'pumped'. The shaft may also be retracted and locked so that the tool can be used as a conventional driver. An added bonus with this tool is that it uses interchangeable bits, which vary for pattern and size.

In contrast, jeweller's screwdrivers are miniature and used for very fine work such as fixing hinges on a dressing box. They do take some dexterity, since the swivelling head is pressured by the index-finger and the grooved shaft is turned with the thumb and free fingers.

I took one tool with me to Spain, a Stanley No. 4 smoothing plane. It had belonged to my grandfather and was as precious to me as his watch box but not terribly useful. Firstly, because it hadn't been used for many years, it was in need of attention. It became evident that my grandfather was no craftsman, the plane never having been fettled[22] for correct use. He was a 'potcher' as they say in the Valleys. He didn't have a clue, really, but he had a go.

"Needs work, but it's okay. It's good quality, at least, and that's worth preserving," Jesús said.

"I want to use it," I said.

"Yes, well, it's good to restore something like this."

Not unreasonably, I thought that engineered tools would be true straight from the box, so was shocked to find that this wasn't the case. Fettling is the process even new planes must go through in order to prepare them for the work for which they are intended. So I had to strip the plane down to its constituent parts. It felt as though I were dismantling a gun as I spread the parts on the bench: body, frog, toe, toat, iron, cap iron, lever cap. And Jesús taught me the names of its parts: lateral blade adjustment lever, chip breaker, mouth, yoke, sole, adjusting knob, heel.

---

[22] The term used to describe how a tool must be modified or adjusted before it is serviceable

I had made up my mind as a child about how I was going to kill them but I did consider other methods of execution over the years. 'Execution', though, suggests a verdict and a sentence, which wasn't quite how I saw it. The concept of justice and the scales above the Old Bailey have always been admirable to me, but it did not – indeed, could not – offer satisfaction.

What the boys did to me – and got away with – would come home to them. Justice – my version of it – must be seen, by me, to be done. Obviously, I considered shooting them with arrows. I had some knowledge of that method. The one (and only) time I'd tried archery I fired an arrow straight through Georgian wired glass[23] and was stunned to note the result: the arrow wagging in the neat hole it had created. I considered, too, the likes of Robin Hood's legendary accuracy, splitting an arrow that was itself dead-centre of the target, and the Welsh bowmen at Agincourt whose bows were so powerful that when the enemy were upon them, arrows went through them into their comrades following behind. As much as I enjoyed the latter and as much as I liked the fact that it would be painful, there was no beauty in it. I concede there is beauty in the bow and, in fact, in the arrows too, but the death is too distant. It could be a very long way away. And besides, Saint Sebastian had been shot with arrows but wasn't killed, eventually being stoned to death. My skill with the bow was well below that necessary for a decent kill, anyway.

A beautiful death is one in which the 'subject' and the instrument are one. The subject is nought without the instrument and the instrument is nought without the subject.

In *The Martyrdom of St. Sebastian* by Andrea Mantegna, Sebastian is just to the left of centre, tied with his back to a column rather than a tree, his eyes lifting heavenward. His torso is particularly beautiful, his muscles well-defined. His robe maintains his privacy but is slung low so that the crease to his groin is teasingly exposed. He prickles with arrows which enter him from all angles.

There are nine arrows but my favourites are the one piercing his

---

[23] The glass one sees in institutions with 'grids' of wire inside it for strength and security

right abdomen and the one passing through his right thigh. The arrows are long and straight. When I visited the painting at the Louvre it was a quiet day. I was able to stand in front of it and take in the figure's majesty. His cheek was good enough to kiss, his brow appealing to my hands to smooth it.

That I didn't kill Bull beautifully was a great disappointment to me. I had started to rehearse the moment of individual deaths not long after I had decided that was what I was going to do. But I failed my first test and I failed Bull. It is important to execute with grace.

He was the third being I had killed (though he was no fish) and had to be the first of the boys because he was, as far as colour and flavour are concerned, my least favourite. I'd categorised him as lemon, the lowest in the hierarchy of the packet: worst was first. So when I caught up with him in his little life, it was a steep learning curve, even though I hate that phrase.

I discovered that Bull with the bull's penis was living in one of the terraces that had been built, in the first instance, for the miners. They were still the staple accommodation of the working class, entirely appropriately, I thought – being stone fronted and square-set – but in order to distinguish themselves from those around them, their windows and doors had been painted in different colours or even replaced altogether with aluminium or plastic. The result had the architectural integrity of a packet of Opal Fruits.

Bull's life consisted of working in a factory by day and drinking heavily in the pub at night. When he entered, his tankard would be taken down from its hook, filled with beer and placed on the bar, all in the time it took to hang up his coat. He must have put on several stone since I'd last seen him. Even if I had wanted to kill him beautifully, I couldn't have. There would be no marriage between him and my love. He was still twp, too, which in some way satisfied me. If he had lost that aspect of his character I might have felt a modicum of regret, which would have disturbed my equilibrium. However, I did use a tool rather than a weapon.

I was deeply depressed after Bull's death. It had been a disaster and I didn't get as far as even introducing him to my darling. It just wouldn't have worked, being neither practical nor aesthetically balanced. It had been physically difficult, nauseating and messy.

Surely a man whose stature not only filled a doorway but made people in the street look behind after he'd passed them, should translate this into a role in life that could accommodate it. But, no. He was a monster carp with a stickleback life. When I found him in the pub he didn't know me. I got talking to him and discovered that he was thick, opinionated and harmless. Nevertheless, there was no question that I would not kill him, though I had not expected him to be so big. So big, in fact, that it would not be possible to include him in my work of art. His death would merely be pragmatic and business-like.

As well as having my beauty in the van, it was more fortunate that I had my tool-box with its basic set. It had been one of the first tasks Jesús had set for me. Although he never went anywhere, he had a travelling box for when he visited clients and had to make adjustments for a piece in situ. I did go places, however, and my tool box was based upon his pattern. It contained one drawer (with dovetailed corners, of course), and a set of tools especially collected for travelling and kept in optimum condition.

When Bull's head slumped, finally, into his supper (black pudding fried up with potato and cabbage) there was no possibility of the beautiful death I had envisaged for him for so many years. He was too big and I had been remiss, failing to take into account that big boys become big men. So I had to improvise. Releasing the catches on the box-front to reveal the contents always stopped my breath, as clichéd as that sounds. It was like that moment when I opened the door to the sitting room (we called it the lounge) on Christmas morning and wondered what was in the darkness, the light switch revealing, suddenly, startling gifts. The Estwing hammer, only ever taken in hand to appreciate its balance, presented itself as the right tool for this particular task. I considered using a screwdriver too but all I had was a cabinet screwdriver, the handle of which is not designed to be struck. There was a chance that it would split or at least be damaged. A plastic fluted-handled screwdriver would have probably sufficed but I disliked them so much that I wouldn't even have one in my kit. Jesús wouldn't have allowed one in the workshop, anyway.

So I opened the drawer to reveal well-proportioned compartments with fixings and small tools. A six-inch oval-headed nail, like a *Rutilus rutilus*[24] whose metallic scales had been forged into a purposeful shaft with head and point, complemented the weight of the hammer in the opposite hand. I lifted Bull's face clear of his plate, which I put to one side, then turned his head so that his left cheek was resting on the kitchen table. I placed the point of the nail in his right ear, held the hammer at the end of the shaft to maximise the transfer of energy from the swing, and struck. Once.

I left the nail in his head and hoped that I would have more luck with orange.

[24] Roach

Chapter Five

The most important book to me at the age of ten was *The Observer's Book of Birds' Eggs.*[25] The first egg in my collection was the speckled *Turdus ericetorum.*[26] The next was *Turdus merula,*[27] usually the first in any boy's collection. Then it was something a little more difficult to acquire, such as *Troglodytes troglodytes*[28] or *Fringilla coelebs,*[29] followed by something almost exotic, like *Gallinula chloropus.*[30] From then it was coveting prizes, species that posed an extra challenge: *Corvus corone,*[31] *Garrulus glandarius.*[32] I studied the eggs minutely in the book. They were illustrations rather than photographs and I was so taken with them that I copied them, making imaginary collections on sheets of paper, juxtaposing the eggs I prized above all others: *Falco tinnunculus,*[33] *Accipiter nisus*[34] and *Buteo buteo.*[35] One boy in the street was given a gull's egg by his uncle. He didn't know what it was and I was able to tell him that it was a *Larus marinus.*[36] It was enormous. I asked the man opposite who raced pigeons for an egg and I passed it off as a *Columba palumbus.*[37]

I was the only one with a book of eggs. The others knew the species through the folklore of older brothers (girls never collected them). My collection was a treasure greater than anything else I possessed (apart from my grandfather's watch box). The eggs nestled in a tin of sawdust and were labelled for a short while, frustratingly and unsatisfactorily. I

[25] Frederick Warne & Co. Ltd., Revised Edition 1954, Eleventh Reprint 1969
[26] Song Thrush
[27] Blackbird
[28] Wren
[29] Chaffinch
[30] Moorhen
[31] Carrion Crow
[32] Jay
[33] Kestrel
[34] Sparrowhawk
[35] Buzzard
[36] Great Black-Backed Gull
[37] Woodpigeon

had wanted the effect of a scholarly museum display like the one I saw at the Natural History Museum on a school trip, but my handwritten labels with a cheap biro on poor quality paper were not quite right. Even then I made the decision that for aesthetic reasons, the visual presence needed balance and cleanliness of expression, so the labels went and the eggs spoke for themselves.

Any species that wasn't local to me was an object of fantasy, like a Fabergé.[38] My locale was the canal, the lanes, the reservoir and the moors on the hills. Occasionally I'd go on what felt like an expedition, combing the hedges and banks, which was rather limiting as far as species were concerned. I wasn't greedy, taking just one for my collection. At school I'd be in class physically but emotionally I'd be on the top of the hill with the wind sweeping my hair across my face or with my fingertips counting the eggs in the soft cup of a *Fringilla coelebs* or the warm mud of a *Pica pica*.[39] Once I took an egg from the nest of *Troglodytes troglodytes* – no mean feat, since the male builds several and the female inspects them to decide which one will be suitable for her brood – to find it cracked. I felt immediately nauseous and tears welled up, but as I swept my finger over it the crack turned out to be just a hair and all was well.

The next hurdle was to blow it without breaking it. I practised on chickens' eggs which, although a good idea, were no preparation for species whose eggs were only as big as the nail on my little finger.

I had been in love with Elena since the age of eleven. I don't suppose it was love then, but it certainly was at the age of fifteen. I'd walk past her house and hope she'd emerge at that moment, be thrilled to see me and invite me in. Ha! There was even the time when I'd acquired a waistcoat and walked past her house, twice, hoping she'd come out and see me, cool (though we didn't say cool, then) with my green combat jacket slung nonchalantly over my shoulder. It was a terrible shock to learn she was 'going out' with Napper. I felt instantly sick. Didn't she know what he was *really* like? Why was it that the 'nice'

---

[38] Peter Carl Fabergé made sixty eight eggs between 1885-1917. They are superb examples of the jeweller's craftsmanship

[39] Magpie

girls went for the horrible boys? It didn't matter, of course, after those boys had finished with me.

I saw her again when I went back. It was strange how it happened. I walked through the village, and it felt as though I hadn't actually noticed some of the places before. I was saddened to discover that the Victorian fencing had been removed from around the park and replaced with a green metal fence that fell short of the original, having neither the presence nor decorative gravitas that a civic fixing should possess. But even before I had set off, I expected to see her. She came out of Kwik Save and walked straight past me so I went after her and tapped her on the shoulder. She recognised me straight away and I was amazed. She asked what I was doing and I just said I was living in Spain, for the moment, but had plans to change direction.

"What do you do, though?" she said.

"Oh, I see. I make things. Furniture. How about you?"

"I work in there," she said, nodding back at Kwik Save. "Married? Kids?" I laughed. "Course not. I forgot."

"It's okay. You?"

"Two boys," she said.

I immediately felt sorry for her.

"But I'm not with the father."

She was lovelier than I remembered. She'd put on weight but still had the most beautiful open features. "Sorry to hear that."

"I was young and he was stupid."

I laughed again.

"You round for long?"

"I'm going back tomorrow."

"Why don't you have my number and next time you come back, we'll go out."

"Yeah."

She took a receipt out of her bag and wrote her number on it. "It's really good to see you," she said, handing it to me.

"We'll do that," I said.

Napper and I had been good friends. I was lucky. If you didn't get on with him, life was difficult. I was left alone. We were both in the athletics team, spending many hours after school, training together, timing each other, egging each other on to do better and better. We were sprinters. We'd sprint and walk back, sprint and walk back, over and over, getting more and more tired, and I would be determined that next time I'd find that extra morsel of strength to beat him. But he beat me by half a yard every time. Then we'd go back to the changing rooms with all the others who'd been doing distance work around the perimeter of the sports fields, or throwing javelins. Or hammers.

There was an inter-schools coming up and extra training had been arranged for the different events. Napper and I turned up for the sprinting and in the showers afterwards he kissed me.

"I *like* you," he said.

I didn't know what to say but stuttered, "I like you, too."

He went to kiss me again but I put my hand against his chest. I got out of the shower and went to dry and dress. He got dressed opposite me but didn't say anything else. Nor did I.

Just as in so many films, I woke up in hospital. It had been difficult for the ambulance crew to reach me, driving as far as they could along the towpath until it became too narrow, then running with their gear and a stretcher. There was a frame over my midriff. The injury, I felt then, would kill me. It didn't, of course, but it might have been better all round if it had done so. The final blow had split my buttocks, smashed my testes and pinned my scrotum to the bolus. In that moment I lost my fatherhood and my libido.

When I discovered that it was Elena who'd found me I felt absolutely torn between thinking she was an angel and mortified that she had seen me naked and broken. She came with her mother to visit me in hospital. She asked me what happened and I said I couldn't remember. The police had asked me the same question and I'd given the same answer. I saw the headlines in the paper: BOY TORTURED. The police appealed for witnesses.

I was the centre of attention for quite some time. The police said I might remember after a while and they kept coming back to question me. They showed me photographs of men, all of whom looked 'odd'.

The surgeons said they could give me new 'balls' when I was older. I wished they hadn't spoken down to me.

Butt Hinges are the traditional choice for furniture and cabinet making. The leaf bearing three 'knuckles' is fixed to the frame and the leaf bearing two 'knuckles' is fixed to the member which moves. Piano hinges – as seen on piano lids – are made in six feet six inch lengths and can be cut to requirements. An extremely pleasing method of support within a piece itself is to cut the hinge out of solid members, known as a Knuckle Joint. These are often found in Pembroke tables where flaps are supported by the underframe's pivoting brackets.

If I could have had a photograph of Elena I would have but I neither had a camera nor an opportunity to take one. No one took a camera to school and how could I have approached her and asked her to pose for a photograph for my gratification? It was all I could do to muster the courage to speak to her. The only time we spoke was in the course of classroom activities, so the only intimacy I shared with her was being in the same room.

I dreamt about her often, invariably wearing a long white cotton nightgown which would be revealed when I pulled back the blankets on her bed. And I would pull the gown up her legs and over her head, her brown skin contrasting against mine, pale and rude it seemed to me.

The dreams were intense and I wanted to enter her so much, wanted to ejaculate inside her, but it never happened. It was what I wanted most of all and even my dreams could not fulfil my needs. Masturbation, however, was not a problem. I masturbated regularly, sometimes three or four times a day, usually in my bedroom or in the bath, imagining myself with Elena in the bedroom scenario, fulfilled or at least, in the world of my head when my eyes were closed. I would masturbate until I hurt myself, occasionally.

Chapter Six

A blunt tool is a dangerous tool. A blunt tool is a lazy tool. It is essential that each one – whether a chisel, plane or saw – is kept at an acceptable level of performance. As soon as a tool dips below this level, it must be sharpened. It is a common experience for the craftsman to think that one more cut with a tool which is not quite sharp may be all that is needed to finish a task but it is risky: it could damage the work and the craftsman. It must never be regarded as a chore but as a habit that is ingrained in the approach to all work. Blunt tools are not tools.

I decided that it was appropriate, in her structure, to use four main species of timber that closely matched lemon, orange, lime and strawberry for colour:

- *Fraximus excelsior*[40]
- *Swietenia macrophylla*[41]
- *Carya illinoensis*[42]
- *Dalbergia frutescens.*[43]

I was particularly pleased with my choice for lime, even though I knew its workability may prove difficult, because it is used for tool handles, especially hammers, sledges and axes. The different characteristics of these timbers would also complement each other and balance the design as a whole. I didn't want to limit myself to these species, however. I had ideas for decorative details in other timbers but I was conscious of not over-doing the design. It's easy to get carried away. In my eagerness to display my skills I had first designed something which did just that at the expense of everything else: it would undoubtedly showcase my ability but it was impractical and lacked poise. I rejected it, eventually, when I came to my senses and realised that it did not fulfil the brief.

---

[40] Ash
[41] Brazilian Mahogany
[42] Hickory
[43] Tulipwood

For example, it had to be transportable. I had to be able to dismantle and reassemble my darling in another location.

There was no doubt that she would be my greatest challenge as a craftsman and my greatest piece. I became obsessed with her and the idea of her. The design, then, took nearly as long as it took for the piece to be made. And once the design was completed, I practised making individual components and joints in softwood species.

Standard spokeshaves, with round or straight faces, cut in a similar manner to bench planes but have narrow soles, which makes them more difficult to use. They take more practice. The best tools are those with an adjustable screw on each corner of the blade with which to precisely set the depth of cut.

There are some awful methods of execution and few of them at all practicable for my purposes. Whilst being broken on the wheel, for example, appealed to my need for revenge, it is extremely violent and un-pretty, a process demanding far too great a contribution from the executioner which, in this case, would be me. And so many of them occurred at a time when the spectacle was as great a form of entertainment as television is to some now, and just as vulgar: boiling alive, burning at the stake, flaying, the gibbet, being hanged, drawn and quartered, the mill wheel, stoning, and tearing apart by two trees. The latter, however, does offer, briefly, to cut out the middle-man craftsman. Why bother converting timber into a piece when one can just use the wood in its natural state? The inherent strength of the wood is the simplest of machines. Two adjacent trees are bound together and then each leg of the victim is tied to each tree. When the rope binding the trees is cut, the trees return to their original position and tear the victim in two. Simple: yes. Pleasing: no. There is no interaction, no balance between the machine and subject, each dependent upon the other for the moment. There is no marriage.

I became obsessed with the notion of a machine that was:
- well designed
- beautifully made
- transportable
- complete when married.

The first thing I killed – which I considered as having a life worth having – was a *Gasterostreus aculeatus*[44]. I caught it with one of those children's nets inserted into the end of a bamboo cane. I placed it on a stone on the towpath and hit it on the head with the handle of my catapult, which I'd seen a man doing on the television to a salmon he'd caught. My 'priest', however, was far too much for the task, and the eyes popped out.

The second thing I killed, entirely accidentally was a *Perca fluviatilis*[45], it having taken my worm deep inside its body, out of sight, rather than being hooked in the lip. In trying to disgorge the hook, blindly, and keeping the tension on the line so that it would come out cleanly, I suddenly strung out the guts between the fish in my left hand and the line in my right.

For Jesús, craftsmanship was a way of life. He would sit with a tool in his hands, contemplating its form and its purpose. He spent many hours ensuring that all of them were ready for use. After each contract was fulfilled he allowed a week in order to ready the workshop for the next. It seemed to me excessive but I came to understand that this was part of the process of making and creativity. Although he would be using the same skills, he needed to prepare himself and his environment for a different piece. He was paid large sums of money. He lived for the love of craftsmanship and this was to become my way of life also.

That we should attend church every Saturday morning allowed him a formal spiritual aspect to his weekly routine. In practice he was more of a Shaker – "Hands to Work, Hearts to God". He had books of furniture design which included Chippendale,[46] and was deeply interested in Arts and Crafts designers, especially Philip Webb, Sir Edwin Lutyens and Charles Rennie Mackintosh.[47] Jesús's drawings were stunning works in themselves and I studied them as

[44] Stickleback
[45] Perch
[46] Jesús had a facsimile of Thomas Chippendale's *The gentleman and cabinet-maker's director: being a large collection of the most elegant and useful designs of household furniture in the Gothic, Chinese and modern taste* (1754)
[47] Especially Webb's *Red House* (1859)

one might study the bible. There were lines and details which I found extraordinarily uplifting and I went to specific drawings for their different effects upon me.

I loved his initial ideas, taped to the top edge of his drawing board, and how these were transformed into designs of exquisite economy. My first drawings were poor, of course, but Jesús would encourage me by singling out a detail which he would then urge me to perfect. But this would be done in my own time because I was his extra pair of hands. When I arrived I only knew the obvious tools, the planes, hammers and saws, but even those I didn't know correctly. I thought I'd arrive, pick up the tools and start producing wonderful things!

Just holding the tools, taking them apart and putting them back together became a spiritual act. I learned by watching Jesús do everything and then being taught explicitly how and why something was done. The tools were the answer to everything: if the tools weren't at an optimum level of performance the craftsman failed in his work and in his life. I remember the first time I tried to sharpen the iron of a No 5½ Jack Plane. Being able to hold the iron at the correct angle[48] on the oilstone while pushing it away and back, and managing to use the whole stone at the same time, was ridiculously difficult. Jesús would not hear of using a honing guide.

"You must be able to feel the grinding angle and raise it to the sharpening angle. A honing guide won't allow you to feel that. You must know the iron itself. You, not a guide, must be responsible for the sharpening."

Sharpening chisels required another way of standing. The stance necessary for sharpening every tool was something I had to train my body and mind to acquire. It reminded me of playing the guitar. When you are learning a new chord your hand has to 'remember' its shape, and over time that is what my body did as I needed to sharpen a particular tool. My body and mind would slot into a half-inch chisel mode, or a block plane iron mode, or panel saw mode (though saws are sharpened using a saw horse). It sometimes felt as though I was part of the tool, I told Jesús.

[48] The grinding angle is 25 degrees, the honing angle is 35 degrees

"That is as important as dreaming in the language that you are learning," he said.

Jesús never reacted to my errors by admonishing me. Rather he would consider whatever it was that had occurred or been caused by me, then help, telling me calmly what I should have done or should do in the future. This was tested to the limit on a day we were working with blonde timbers. I was paring the shoulder of a tenon when the one-inch chisel I was using slipped and sliced through the knuckle over the index-finger of my left hand, staining the workface with blood. He took my arm and led me to the sink immediately and washed the wound under cold water. Then he made butterfly stitches, expertly, out of a strip of plaster, binding the clean edges against each other.

"This is what happens when you use a blunt tool," he said.

The blood in the timber wouldn't have mattered were it not for the fact that it had seeped into the grain and there was no leeway in the dimensions of the timber, which was already at its finished measurements. I had to make a new member from scratch.

"You'll live," he said.

I enjoyed Jesús caring for me like this. He did everything so well.

After church one Saturday, Jesús and I went to the *Café del Mar* for lunch. I had a chorizo sandwich and Jesús had tortilla. I liked the way coffee was served in small glass tumblers. All of the cafés in the city appeared to have their own quirk, apart from the two very large ones, the *San Miguel* and *Dindurra*. They had a loyal clientele that changed and shifted according to the time and day. In the morning there would be a variety of workers taking breakfast; women would meet mid-morning to share the foibles of their children, or husbands, or both; old and retired men would set up their chess sets and play against each other late in the afternoon; young couples arrived mid-evening, feeding each other morsels of food. On Saturday and Sunday afternoons whole families arrived and took up several tables, the waiters pirouetting around them.

Gregorio had The ODJB[49] playing through the speakers.

[49] The Original Dixie Land Jazz Band

Jesús looked out over the harbour: "*Porque de tal manera amós Dios al mundo, que la dado á su Hijo unigénito, para que todo aquel que en él cree, no se pierda, mas tenga vida eternal,*"[50] he said. That was all. He was still in church.

I sipped my coffee and looked at the yachts in the harbour, their flags and home ports meaning something to somebody.

"I used to wonder about having a son," Jesús said. "I've always wanted to have a boy to pass on my skills. I didn't expect someone as old as you, who needed to be shown everything from the start, but I'm pleased with how you've developed."

For a man who mostly communicated by a nod or a shake of the head, he was practically garrulous.

"I love what I'm doing," I said. "Everything."

He nodded. And that was our conversation for the whole day.

I had put so much into the design and making of my sweet that I had lost sight of the contribution of those individuals for whom I had designed her. I was eager to see her perform and had spent so many hours making her portable, that I had not considered a simple variable when it came to killing Bull: big boys become big men. That was such an oversight that I had to go back to the drawing board – literally. It was an excuse to reconsider the design and ensure that my darling could cope with Ev, Dog and Napper, however large they had become. The modifications weren't a chore, rather a reconfiguration of the proportions, having discovered that not every context had been considered. Putting my darling together within the sterility of the workshop was bound to affect her performance. She was going to love the boys in a context completely foreign to her surroundings and didn't know, precisely, where and when she would come to life.

The modifications were quite lovely, allowing me to indulge in secret dovetails in sparkling *Acer pseudoplatanus.*[51]

---

[50] 'For God so loved the world that he gave His only-begotten Son, so that whoever believes in Him should not perish, but have everlasting life'. John 3:16
[51] European Sycamore

Changing my name was the natural action to undertake: I left behind the world I'd belonged to and took up membership of another. When I woke up in hospital to discover that I had been changed, radically, I began to plan the new me. I believed that I'd left as one person and would return as another. It was essential, though, that the name swelled with each facet of my new self. I'd spend long periods of time considering names as if I were trying on a new coat. Nothing was quite appropriate: too heavy, too thin, too short. It struck me as so obvious once I realised what it should be that it was a moment of profound relief as well as disappointment that I hadn't seen it before: Sebastian. I had been looking at a pen and brown ink drawing of Sebastian with the aid of a large magnifying glass in the drawings collection at the *Biblioteca Ambrosiana*.[52] Although tiny,[53] it was a marvel of proportion by a brilliant hand. I loved the way the head tilted and the depiction of the testicles as one round ball. It would have been a lovely object to keep in my grandfather's box.

I decided to make a pair of doors with raised and fielded panels in *Acer saccharum*[54] with a haunched mortise and tenon frame in *Juglans regia*.[55] The fittings I chose to complement the timbers were bronze, including the hinges. I honed my one-inch chisel until I created the finest of burrs, flattened it off and stropped it on my hand. Some craftsmen use a piece of leather but Jesús wouldn't hear of it: "Leather is skin," he said, "use your own." To see him stropping chisels or plain irons was amazing because of the speed and the noise it made. He showed me how to do it, slowly, but still I managed to nick my hand the first time.

Having marked the position of the hinges with a small engineer's square and a pin-sharp 4H pencil, I placed the newly honed chisel just shy of the line and punched it into the grain with the *Lignum vitae* carving mallet. It was a memorable moment: the precision of a sharp chisel is a source of joy.

[52] Piazza Pio Xl, Milan, Italy
[53] 2 5/16" x 7/8"
[54] Hard Maple
[55] European Walnut

Georgian and Victorian box sash windows use a very simple pulley wheel system over which lead weights counterbalance the weight of the sash. The correct leads ensure that a sash can be raised or lowered with ease. It was a technique that I decided to utilise in my darling. Her seat – which I was going to carve out of elm similar to those of traditional English Windsor chairs – would slide in its groove and be positioned and held wherever I chose. But as soon as I released the lock, and the weight of the sitter was added, one of my darling's surprises would manifest itself through the aperture in the seat. I had considered carefully and at great length the surprise that Jesús had proferred – that of an aesthetic one – and there were plenty of these, but I also had to incorporate surprises that were purely functional and utilitarian. Killing someone is, simply expressed, mundane. Killing someone beautifully takes craftsmanship.

Because I had to be able to dismantle her, it was necessary to incorporate some joints that were strong yet practical i.e. suitable to be taken apart. A loose-wedged mortise and tenon joint – which is used often in refectory tables – is fit for such a purpose, but I planned to use the Tusk Tenon, a variation used by carpenters to join floor joists, which has an additional stubbed tenon (the tusk) for extra support. She needed this strength.

But I was keen, also, to showcase my skills (at least to myself) so wanted to use every dovetail joint that it was possible to incorporate:
- through dovetail
- decorative through dovetail
- rebated through dovetail
- lapped dovetail
- double lapped dovetail
- secret mitred dovetail (already incorporated)
- bevelled dovetail.

Chapter Seven

It wounded me when I saw Napper and Elena holding hands. I was on the canal with my grandfather's binoculars (embarrassingly old but better than nothing) watching a *Muscicapa striata*[56] going to and from its nest, when they appeared around the bend swinging their hands between them, a guitar slung over Napper's back like a gun. My stomach turned over: what was she doing with *him*? He wasn't even part of the group to which she belonged. He was part of a different set altogether, and within that group, a specific faction. Whichever faction you looked at, however, each would comfortably fall into the category of moronic. The contents of my stomach suddenly transformed into foreign food and my bowels turned to water.

Napper pulled Elena closer to himself as they approached and put his arm around her neck, turning her head to kiss her lovely mouth, the lips I had kissed in my dreams and wished now, madly, were being pressed against mine, there, beneath the arching *Quercus robur* and *Fagus sylvatica* next to the still water of the canal with *Sylvia atricapilla*[57] singing summer in the low branches.

I wanted to tell her, *Look, he's bad, he's a bully,* I *hate him, everyone hates him, he's been spoiled, he gets everything he wants.* And at that moment he had what – who – I wanted: a graceful, clean-faced, elegant angel walking towards me with the sun behind her, causing her hair to glow at the edges like a nimbus.

"All right, Tim," Elena said.

"Yes thanks."

"Seen any sparrows?" Napper said.

I wanted to smash him in the face. *"Passer domesticus, Passer montanus*[58] or *Prunella modularis?"*

"Oh fuck off, twat!"

Elena pushed him. He laughed one of those laughs girls found so endearing and which I found stupid. Don't fall for that, I wanted to

---

[56] Spotted Flycatcher
[57] Blackcap
[58] Tree Sparrow

say. Don't fall for anything. But nothing Elena did could taint her in my eyes. It was something over which she had no control and which I couldn't understand.

"Come on," she said, pulling him away, "we're spoiling his fun. See you Tim."

He was laughing and he went along with her. He swung his guitar from around his back and made as if to shoot me with it. As they walked away he flicked a 'V' behind his back.

When working in fine timbers it is important to mark constituent members accurately. The rule is to mark twice and cut once i.e. check the measurements before committing to the cut. Accuracy is achieved, firstly, in the scale drawings and rods drawn full-size on sheets of hardboard or ply. These lines are then transferred to the timber.

It is also important to use the pencil that is most suitable. A carpenter's pencil, with its thick wide lead, is really only useful for large work where tolerances are less crucial. To ensure accuracy the pencil line must be fine, so a soft lead with its quickly thickening line is best kept for sketching initial ideas. Hard leads produce a fine line and keep their points. A good pencil is 4H, the line of which is still dark enough to see clearly on dark timbers. Pencils must be regarded with the same integrity as any other tool: buy the best. A craftsman cannot make quality pieces unless the marking out is accurate.

I remember the woodwork teacher knocking the top and bottom rails of a cot side together in the workshop. It was very odd to me, not having a younger sibling and having no memory of a cot of my own, but when I lay in the hospital bed contemplating my new self, it began to trouble me that this sphere would be one I would never experience. It hurt. And the hurt worsened over time.

My injuries were horrific. The prognosis – beyond the immediate and detached medical jargon – was that I would never be a father.

Opal Fruits were launched onto the market in 1971. They were *made to make your mouth water*. I wasn't one of those people who ate the sweets as they presented themselves; I discarded the paper packet and stacked up the flavours, eating lemon first, then lime, followed by orange and strawberry. I saved the best until last. Having a whole packet to myself was heavenly. I used to think, Why don't they make packets of individual flavours? Imagine, a whole packet of strawberry!

I ran my life strictly, for a while, according to the hierarchy of Opal Fruits. I would consider all manner of things and award them colours that would effectively categorise them as good or bad. So I would be out watching birds and if I saw *Passer domesticus* I'd think – lemon, and if I saw *Accipiter nisus* I'd think – strawberry. I needed another flavour for *Falco peregrinus* but I would think 'strawberry-plus' or 'strawberry-plus-plus'. I had never seen one. That would have been superlative.

The Wizard of Oz would be lemon, definitely, *Oliver Twist* strawberry. *The Bridge on the River Kwai* – lime. *The Great Escape* – orange. *Great Expectations* – with its fantastic opening on the marshes, poor Magwitch the scariest person I'd ever seen and a victim of his surroundings[59] – strawberry too. In one sense, I was a modern-day Magwitch. How ironic that I should be so abused against that living thing, wood, which would be what I loved most, facturing its form and characteristics into something beautiful and functional. In hospital I decided that I would forgive the *Quercus robur* to which I had been tied, using the notion of its strength and beauty to exonerate its part in my metamorphosis.

It is essential to maintain accuracy when cutting the pencil lines of joints marked on timber. This is achieved by placing a try square along the line – the shoulder of a tenon, for example – and cutting the line with a marking knife (some craftsmen use a craft knife). This breaks the grain before a saw is used to perform the main cut and ensures a clean face to the shoulder. It is important to split the grain cleanly so that when the saw is used there is no splaying out that could

---

[59] "A man with no hat, and with broken shoes, and with an old rag tied round his head. A man who had been soaked in water, and smothered in mud, and lamed by stones, and cut by flints, and stung by nettles, and torn by briars; who limped and shivered, and glared and growled…" *Great Expectations* (1861)

mar the face of the work. The saws used for cutting joints in fine furniture tend to be those with a fine tooth-set, anyway, back saws with shorter and stiffer blades than panel saws. If a housing is to be cut, then the same procedure must be followed, cutting the housing lines with a knife first, sawing and then chopping out, finishing to depth with a router.

I had always maintained that I could not remember anything about what had happened to me. I was diagnosed as having been so traumatised that my mind had compartmentalised the event and buried it like a time capsule. If I had ever said who was responsible I would never have had the satisfaction of killing them one by one, or the making of my darling, and my *raison d'être* would have disintegrated. There would have been a trial and I would have had to stand in the witness box. My body would have been presented as evidence to the court. Bull, Ev, Dog and Napper would have enjoyed the limelight. And I would have lost, again.

I had lost every time and I wanted to win. However long it took. I had the patience. Ever since I had spent a whole day fishing for a *Cyprinos carpio*[60] just like that I had watched a man landing the evening before in the same spot, I realised I could wait for what I wanted, forever, if necessary. Its scales glowed like pearls along its sides, its big mouth and gills gaped, and I had the intense rush of grace as I cupped its girth in the water before releasing it.

The modern router machine can perform an astonishing number of tasks with extraordinary accuracy and impressive finish. Because the bits spin at such high revolution, the cuts are wonderfully clean. They have become essential tools in the contemporary workshop, their versatility saving time and money. But there is still a place for the combination plane in the serious craftsman's workshop, often being quicker to set up and use than the machine. As its name suggests, it is capable of performing a multiplicity of tasks, including rebating, grooving, fluting and reeding, as well as creating a variety of decorative mouldings. It is pleasing to experience the cutting process manually, where the power is provided by the craftsman rather than an electrical motor. It is a further example of

[60] Mirror Carp

the craftsman's skill that the correct pressure, rhythm and speed are applied to achieve the optimum performance from the tool. A machine, in contrast, merely has to be guided.

Chapter Eight

For someone who knew birds' names inside out, I was ignorant when I saw the chickens Jesús allowed to run around. But to call them chickens was as annoying as someone describing any white seabird as a seagull. What *kind* of chicken? Jesús put me right: "The one with the rose comb is a Leghorn. Lovely white eggs and lots of them. The blue-grey bird is an Araucana, another good layer with fabulous blue-green eggs – and the blue-black banded one is a Maran, eggs dark brown."

I became instantly fond of them all. Occasionally an egg would still be warm when I collected it. A perfect design, with no joins of any kind.

Even though I had not collected wild birds' eggs for many years, I still derived enormous pleasure from seeing them, so I made nesting boxes out of scraps in the workshop in order to encourage *Parus caeruleus, Erithacus rubecula* and *Turdus merula* which had territories around the house. I made a box, too, for *Tyto alba*,[61] which I had heard in the copse at the edge of the field. They weren't like the boxes that could be purchased through the RSPB, butt-jointed and nailed like a handyman, but boasted fine woodworking skills. They were an excuse for me to try out my ideas for my darling to see if they were suitable and whether I could perform them successfully.

Jesús was amused, I think, and when the boxes were occupied he nodded and raised his eyebrows in approval. A Robin became a friend, appearing in the doorway and on the window-sill of the workshop and kitchen. I saw Jesús toss a worm to it one day and it pleased me. When a pair of *Tyto alba* began using the box I collected their pellets and dissected them. I would use a pair of tweezers to pick them apart, separating the hair from the bones to identify the small animal the digestive processes had unmade. The bones were small and delicate and I arranged the skeletons on board and glued them in place, creating museum-like displays in simple frames of ebony, which I hung in the

---

61 Barn Owl

49

workshop. It was relevant, after all, being the underlying structure of the animal's being, just like the pieces we were producing. The joints fascinated me, not least because they must have been supported by muscles and tendons which could not be replicated in my darling. Besides, I wanted to create something which functioned as timber as far as practicable.

The ball and socket joint of our own skeletons – at the shoulder – allowed movement in a variety of planes. I had believed it impossible from a strictly furniture-making perspective, but realised that if I selected a species that was suitably durable, it *could* be achieved. It would be easiest to use a lathe, which Jesús wouldn't allow and which I was loath to do. So I carved the ball and socket by hand in *lignum vitae*[62] using spokeshaves and gouges to create two astonishing joints which, when combined with the counterbalancing weights, provided aesthetically profound and lethal surprises.

Killing Dog was successful, partially. It was certainly better than having to hammer something into his head as I had done with Bull. My darling – through no fault of her own – performed respectably given the context, but there were problems.

Dog had achieved a better position than Bull. I caught up with him in a detached house spectacularly upmarket from the two-bedroomed terrace of his childhood. It was 'detached' in the sense that there were a few feet, at least, between it and the houses either side, one of its three bedrooms over a garage. It had the architectural beauty of a box of matches. All mod cons. Carpets. Plastic windows. Everything necessary for a double-glazed life. Considering my enormous disgust, it was apt that I should kill him in the sitting room, especially because there was a sheet of glass and a piece of hardboard which passed for a frame, within which a poster of a fast car[63] had been sandwiched.

---

[62] Extremely durable since it is often used for lock-gates

[63] I cannot describe it, apart from the fact that it was red. I have always hated cars and so know nothing about them. I presume it was something special because it was on display. I am not averse to the beauty of machines, of course, and have always found Jesús's Citroën Traction Avant an elegant presence on the road

I broke the egg of a Maran into the pan and my eyes were drawn at once to the yolk's bulging flash upwards, then the seismic albumen skirting outwards with a sizzle. This is how it would be when Napper and my sweet invention consummated their marriage. A nuclear event. *The* moment.

I am sure I am not the only person to have cringed when their name was called out in school, whatever the reason. Everyone else's name always sounded appropriate for them. I would look at someone and think, *Well of course that's Matthew Rand, there's no one else it* could *be*, for example. But mine crucified me: Tim. I hadn't even been given the opportunity of being able to call myself Timothy, thereby augmenting my presence. Tim. Three phonemes[64] – [t], [ɪ] and [m] which created a monosyllabic sound-print. Tim. A print that was barely noticeable, with its voiceless alveolar plosive,[65] miniscule vowel and voiced bilabial[66] which switched off the light and closed the door behind it.

So it was with great relief that I learned that I could change it to something with substantially more presence: Sebastian, which I pronounced with four syllables and a wonderfully plosive bilabial [b]. In English, at least. In Spain I was Sebasti-*A*no, the [a:] vowel pouncing on the nasal alveolar [n][67] like a big beast. 'Bastian' made me think of 'bastion', that projection from a fortification, a castle, implying strength and power. It was like having protective shields all around me, much like a Roman 'turtle'.[68]

My favourite place in Salamanca was Café Jazz. It was large and open and full of students, not just from Spain, but from all over the world.

---

[64] Phoneme – the smallest distinct segment of sound in a language
[65] The 't' consonant at the beginning of the name. It describes the place of articulation in the mouth, the tongue touching the alveolar ridge behind the teeth
[66] The 'm' consonant. Produced with both lips touching and the voice 'behind' it
[67] These symbols are used in the International Phonetic Alphabet to describe the sounds of individual phonemes
[68] When a group of Roman soldiers came under attack from archers, they would protect themselves on all sides by taking cover behind their shields so that they resembled the shell of a turtle

It had been a shock to begin with, one of the most beautiful cities in Europe. Cafés spilled across the Plaza Mayor. It seemed a strange clash of the beautiful and the everyday at first, as I enjoyed a coffee and watched a man pull down the trousers of his young son so that he could urinate in a drain. And outside Café Jazz an old man with a grey beard sold books of his own poetry opposite two men selling trinkets, badges and drug paraphernalia from a small table.

My time passed here trying not to fall in love with a girl from New York, which if my knowledge of the place from Hollywood films would have me believe, was the scariest place in the civilised world. I had to keep in mind how silly this notion was. If Americans' only knowledge of Wales was John Ford's *How Green Was My Valley*,[69] then their impression was of miners walking home from their shift singing in four-part harmony.

My experience of Americans was non-existent. They were rare in the Valleys. When I was a child there was a TV programme which began with fireworks exploding over Disneyland's skyline. It was beyond anything I could then have hoped to experience. To meet a real person who spoke with an American accent was therefore, even as an adult, extraordinary. There were many in Salamanca, though, studying in the universities, and Café Jazz was the 'cool' place to be.

The clientele was definitely young and I had stumbled upon the place, attracted by the open doors and music. Rather than sit at a table, I went to a stool at the bar and took in the surroundings, partly by looking in the mirror on the back wall. There I was, sipping espresso from a small cup, an inadequate reflection of me.

She came in with a small group of friends who were immediately hailed by a group at the back of the café, unaware that she bumped me as I held the cup to my mouth. She made a fuss, then, putting her hand on my shoulder and apologising profusely in Spanish.

"It's okay," I said.

"Oh you're English."

---

[69] With Walter Pidgeon, Maureen O'Hara, Donald Crisp and Roddy McDowall. It won the Oscar for Best Film in 1941, defeating Orson Welles's *Citizen Kane* and John Huston's *The Maltese Falcon*

I'd been here before. Everyone assumed I was English. When I said Welsh, they usually looked perplexed, so I went along with it. I registered her beauty in a matter of fact way, because I knew there was nothing I could do about it. It was never something I could act upon: yes she was beautiful, no I couldn't 'go' there.

"I'm Stacey," she said, offering her hand, small and warm and fine in my hand. "You a student?"

"You could say that."

"Is that a yes or a no?"

"Yes, a student. You?"

"Got it in one. What are you studying?"

"Furniture design."

"Oh I didn't know they did that here."

"I didn't say where I was doing it."

She laughed. "What can I get you?"

"I didn't spill my drink."

"I know. I just want to apologise, that's all."

She ordered another coffee and a beer.

"What do you drive?" had been Dog's opener.

"I'm sorry?"

"You must drive. What do you drive?"

I was acquainted well enough, by then, to say confidently, "The HY out there."

"A what? Never heard of it."

"It's a Citroën."

"Yeah I saw the washboard on wheels thing, but what do you *drive*?"

"That's it. Nothing else. That's what I drive. Oh, and sometimes I drive a Traction Avant."

"Oh, you don't want to bother with those bloody things. Nothing but trouble, Citroëns. Far too bloody quirky. What you want is a Beamer for work and a Porsche for the weekend."

"Good, are they?"

"You're pulling my pisser," he said.

"No I'm not."

53

"You are, you are. A BMW for work and a Porsche for play."

"Ah," I said, "I don't know much about cars."

"Everyone knows about cars. A 911, that's what you want. Sheer bloody craftsmanship."

"I am a craftsman," I said, and felt physically enlarged saying so. "I make fine furniture."

"I like a good bit of craftsmanship," he said.

"I have a piece with me, if you'd like to see it."

Her wings were the first thing Dog noticed.

"They're smart," he said.

He smoked cigarillos now, large ones which he allowed to dangle from the corner of his mouth or held, just as he had held cigarettes all those years ago, cupped in his hand as if to hide them.

I had brought her into his house and set her up, putting the warehouse-bought furniture against the walls to give her enough room. She looked uncomfortable, her quality screaming to be in a grand atrium. It was like putting a Chippendale chair in a greasy spoon café.

"Aren't they?" I said. "An indulgence I made from Sycamore which I had to steam and laminate to shape."

"Smart," he said again.

It was what a man who likes cars *would* say. He recognised that there was something special about the wings but had no lexis with which to express it. But I wasn't there to concern myself with his shortcomings. He had, however, highlighted an aesthetic concern: there *was* something about the wings which needed my attention.

The problem with the wings distracted me from my purpose momentarily, and I made a mental note to consider it when I returned to Spain. In the instant between Dog taking his place on the seat and it taking his weight, I was struck by the quality of the craftsmanship. For what felt like an awful tranche of time before the weights registered his presence, I thought my darling was going to fail, but as soon as the weight had balanced, the surprises manifested themselves. The only evidence of this was the sound, which resembled that of a sharp plane iron taking a fine shaving from a length of timber, and the blood which appeared from his mouth.

But when I took Dog off the seat I found him to be stuck: the surprise that had risen through the *Ulmus procera*[70] had jammed and I had to pull him off it, damaging my darling in the process. The sound of my darling's performance had lifted my spirits to an extraordinary height and I walked all around her to view her from every angle. Dog, sitting there with his mouth open, was perfect and dumb, though I half expected the song of *Chloris chloris* to start suddenly. That he was stuck sent me into a spiral of despair. I wanted to smash his head in, at first, before I realised that it was all my doing – my skills had to be confirmed, still. I felt so bad that I wished I *had* used a bow and arrow.

[70] English Elm

Chapter Nine

Sharpening a panel saw takes patience. First, the saw has to be clamped in a 'saw-horse'. Then each tooth is sharpened individually with a saw file, whose triangular cross-section fits between the teeth. Once each tooth has been sharpened along one edge, the saw (or the 'saw-horse') is turned around and the process is repeated.

Finally, the teeth have to be aligned with a saw-set, a tool similar to a pair of pliers which 'pushes' each tooth into its correct position. Again, it is necessary to carry out this procedure first along one set of teeth, then the other.

Spending money was difficult. It would take me an inordinate amount of time to decide which of the floats on the rack in Woolworth's would be suitable for my needs. I used a peculiar formula which consisted of its shape, colour, weight, imagining what it would look like in the water, how it would behave and, of course, the price. A similar self-torture would be endured when choosing a new pencil, also, and whatever anyone thought of me as I tried each pencil in my hand, the process ensured that whatever I did purchase, eventually, would be treasured. Losing a piece of tackle in a tree or on something submerged was tragic. If anyone borrowed a pencil in Art, my lesson would be ruined, since I would spend the whole class reminding myself to ask for its return at the end.

I presume it is similar to what amputees must feel, thinking they still have the limb they have lost. There was a strange absence of weight the first time I stood up, and when I first wore underpants again, the usual habit of adjusting my scrotum and testes in order not to pinch them was entirely habitual. The pants didn't 'feel' right. In some ways it felt as though I should be wearing knickers, except I had a penis to support, still.

The doctors were concerned about 'erectile function' and 'libido' though they couched this in terms of erections only. When the surgeon first asked me whether I had had any erections since I had been in hospital, I looked at him perplexed.

"A boner," he said, as if I didn't understand, "a hard-on?" I just wasn't expecting him to ask, that's all.

"No."

"Early days, yet. It may take a little while."

I held on to that, thinking each day could be the day when I had such a powerful erection that I needed to masturbate to relieve the tension.

The nurse pulled back the sheet and the surgeon carefully took off the dressing to examine my wound. I had never had anyone look at me like this. Altogether, there were the surgeon, the nurse and three junior doctors looking at my balls, or lack of them.

"It looks very good," the surgeon said. "It's very neat. No sign of infection. Very good." He turned to the juniors. "Take a look."

Each of them approached. Only one of them looked at me and smiled, nodded, and raised her eyebrows as if to agree.

"I don't want you to worry about this," the surgeon continued. "There are things we can do for you. Give this time to heal and mend and we'll have you back in."

At that point I didn't quite understand but said, "Thank you," inanely, quite overwhelmed by women looking at my penis with no balls.

Cabinet scrapers are thin pieces of metal which are used to take extremely fine shavings from surfaces. Prepared correctly, they can remove the slightest blemishes. The standard square cut scrapers can be used just with the craftsman's hands, or they can be mounted in a purpose-made tool (which resembles a spokeshave) called a scraper plane, with a screw positioned behind the centre of the blade, freeing the craftsman to concentrate on controlling the tool. Bending the scraper into a curve with the hands can be hard work, and the scraper gets hot enough to burn if used over longer periods, so the scraper plane is worth purchasing if you use it often. The finish created can be superb and prepares the surface for final finishing. As well as the basic rectangular scraper, there are goose-neck and concave/convex shapes which are used for finishing mouldings or other shaped surfaces.

It was generous but typical of Elena to give me a copy of *Birds' Eggs and Nests: A Concise Guide in Colour*[71] when she visited me.

"It's wonderful," I said, my eyes filling so that I couldn't see the pages clearly as I flicked through it, before my eyes couldn't hold any more and the tears bomped[72] down my face.

Elena held my hand and I loved her so much then that I believed I would never love as much again.

"I'll go and get a cuppa," her mother said, quietly.

"I thought you'd like it," Elena said.

"It's brilliant."

"It's okay then?"

I nodded a little too vigorously.

We didn't speak for a while then I said, "I'm sorry."

"What for?"

"Um," I didn't know. It was something to do with her finding me.

"There's nothing to be sorry about."

"But...."

More silence. I didn't know what to say. What *could* I say? *You saw me naked. I want to see you naked. I dream about you all the time. I want to make love with you. You are beautiful and I want to treasure you.* The freckles sprinkled on her nose were as perfect as the markings on the egg of a *Turdus viscivorus*.

"You look much better than when I found you."

I felt myself blush.

"You're going to be fine," she said, as if repeating something an adult had said.

"Thank you for helping me."

"Anyone would have done the same."

I said, after a while, "No they wouldn't."

Elena was always very kind to me after that and I even went to her house for tea. We had burgers, chips, peas and ice-cream for dessert.

---

[71] By Jan Hanzák & illustrated by Premysl Pospísil and Miroslav Rada. Published 1971, reprinted 1973. Hamlyn. Translated by Margot Schierlová

[72] South Wales dialect for 'heavily' or 'copiously'

I fantasized that I was her boyfriend and wanted to go upstairs and see her in the white gown I dreamed about. But while I was there the phone rang and her mother called her away to talk to 'Matt'. I had been enjoying this but she visibly lit up when that name was uttered. I thought, *He's just going to use you as a mat.* The fact that he was taking her away from me, even there, angered me, and though I realised she was besotted, I was not going to be dissuaded from the goal I had set for myself.

I no longer registered on their radar. I'd been in school a week and I wasn't aware that they had recognised the fact, but when I went into the toilets at break-time, Ev appeared at the side of me when I was washing my hands.[73]

"So, you're trying to nick Napper's girlfriend?" he said.

"Eh?"

"You might lose something else, if you're not careful."

It was my first indication that *everyone* knew what I had lost.

"I don't remember what happened," I said.

"Lost your memory as well?"

"That's what the doctors say."

"Permanent, is it?"

"They don't know."

"But *you* know," he said.

Yes, I knew, I knew everything. I knew that I would never make love to Elena. I knew that he would be orange. I knew that I would kill him. "I know nothing," I said.

"Good." And he dropped his hand heavily on my shoulder before he walked out.

It might sound preposterous, but I wasn't aware of the *Quercus robur* to which I had been tied the first time I walked past it after the event. I was busy looking at the water, looking for a good spot. The water changed from day to day and reeds or patches of weed would appear,

---

[73] I was the only boy I knew who *did* wash his hands. Everyone else went in there to relieve themselves and go straight out. If they were older, they quickly checked their hair in the mirror first. Or they smoked

creating likely habitats for fish. Trees would suddenly present an area of shade imperceptibly, their leaves stretching out and weighing down branches overnight, just that little extra necessary for a perfect environment in which to set my float. I particularly enjoyed the skill required to cast under low branches, even though there was a risk of losing tackle, or, indeed, because of such a risk: to place the float just where I wanted, having avoided the obstacles, made the catch I hoped for even sweeter.

When the saw blade is 'sighted' from the handle to the tip, the newly set teeth will create a 'V' down its length. If the blade is perfectly true, it should be possible to lay a fine needle in the 'set', lift the saw slightly and watch it travel the length of the blade without faltering.

Chapter Ten

If I had made something which people recognised, then they would call it a chair. Pressed to decide on its nomenclature, I would call it an angel, which for me was a cross between a person and a bird. It – or 'she', as I preferred – would kill with grace and precision. The wings of my darling – my angel – however, were not sufficiently angelic: buzzards are not a species one might regard as representative of heaven. They are essentially crows with hooked beaks, feeding on carrion most of the time and taking rabbits occasionally. A swan might be considered angelic, with wide white wings, which always looked graceful when being flexed. But a swan trying to get airborne, or, indeed, coming to land, looks as graceful as a hastily developed bomber of World War Two. The buzzard soars on outstretched wings and in this aspect is the most graceful of flyers. The first time I saw one I followed its sound, leaving the marked path in Craig-y-Merchant, up a bank of thick brush until I came out at a fence and an open field. There were two buzzards, in fact, circling and mewing. I went to school next day and, while the English teacher talked around some trifling point, I comforted myself with the memory of those buzzards. They were calling for me.

I started carrying a profile gauge when I was transfixed by the moulding of an architrave around a doorway in *The Hotel Lido* in Venice but was unable to copy it. Since then I have pressed my gauge against mouldings in all sorts of places and on all sorts of things, from a dado rail in Florian's[74] to the foot of a marble column in the National Gallery, from a chair in Café Bloom in Amsterdam to a desk in the Chrysler Building, New York. It allowed me to transfer a profile immediately to a piece of paper which could then be kept on record and, if need be, replicated in the workshop. What began as an idiosyncrasy of my travel baggage became my camera, taking snaps of the vernacular. I filed them all, categorising them according to the country, context and type.

---

[74] The historical café in Piazza San Marco, Venice

Angels in paintings are always rather odd figures, children or trumpeting adults, their proportions quite unsuitable for my purposes. My angel had to be able to take a person's breath away.

For a time I called her Est because I was thinking of her as my dearest and sweetest, as in dear-Est and sweet-Est and loveli-Est. It might have been a reaction to what I believed her 'subjects' would think of her when they met, that I was trying to name her. It was ultimately unsatisfactory. She couldn't carry a name. Angel was just one of the ways I thought of her in the time it took me to conceive of, and create her: she was my Red Kite and my rising sun, my *paloma blanca* and my precious Prado,[75] my Great Grey Shrike[76] and my River Usk. There were times when her beauty and her presence and her lines even took *me* by surprise. Whenever she was in mind, however, she was always my darling. My darling angel. Dearest, sweetest, loveliest darling. Darling *darling* darling. Est est est.

When I returned to Spain I put my love back together and tested her. She stuck, again and again, and I could not understand why, since I had tested her before leaving and she had worked perfectly. I left her in the workshop for a week, puzzling over the problem, busying myself with bird boxes and a commission. When I got back to her, I discovered that she worked again perfectly. The components had stuck because the atmospherics in Wales were different, causing joints and timbers to swell, and the relatively tiny increments in size had caused my pleasure to be quashed. Any type of swelling could be catastrophic because the tolerances to which I worked were so fine.

The surprise in the seat had to be presented in a different manner. It meant I had to re-design this aspect completely, so that sticking would not occur. I had to test it in various atmospherics, so I built a cupboard which was capable of creating a variety of conditions. It took months to perfect my darling so that she would be able to perform in whatever climate was expected. I began by renewing the components of the seat altogether. That proved to be an idea for

---

[75] One of the world's great museums, Madrid

[76] *Lanius excubitor*, sometimes known as "the butcher bird" because of its penchant for impaling its prey on thorns or barbed wire

which I could think of no other adjective than 'silly'. Just re-making the components wasn't going to help – though I did complete them with more finesse than previously. I should have realised that I needed to re-design from the outset. Not that it was in any way onerous. In my most positive moments I was able to tell myself that, although my darling had not performed as well as she ought to have, I had fulfilled half of what I had set out to achieve: I *had* killed Dog. I had not killed him beautifully.

I spent a great deal of time in Café del Mar with my notebook and pencils, watching the yachts coming and going. I had wondered, more than once, whether it would be possible to get my darling to sail across the sea but the logistics soon defeated me. Every modicum of space on a yacht is for the yacht itself and anything extraneous would be an outrageous luxury. The only boats that could have accommodated her were huge cruisers and such vessels were out of the question. So I transported her in a van in which she could be packed without her being bruised by the roads or my driving.

I also wondered whether it made any difference to Bull and Dog that they had not died as I had intended. Where were they?

I was twelve years old when I first saw *A Matter of Life and Death*.[77] I was completely taken with its central premise, that when your time is up you have to go and getting out of it is very difficult indeed. I was certain that Bull and Dog experienced nothing as fantastic as an angel being sent to collect them. It wasn't as if either of them had injuries from which they could have recovered! Nevertheless, I did begin to think they had made – or were making – a journey. But to where, exactly? I wondered if I had actually created a version of Wells's machine.[78] They must be somewhere. That space they had taken up – the air they had displaced, even – could not merely disappear. They had to

---

[77] The film by Michael Powell and Emeric Pressburger (1946). David Niven is a bomber pilot who fails to reach heaven when he bails out of his stricken plane without a parachute. When heaven realises that he has not turned up, an angel is sent to find him. Heaven is shot in monochrome and earth in Technicolor

[78] H. G. Wells, author of *The Time Machine*

be *somewhere*. But I wasn't at all sure if they would exist in black and white or colour.

It is important for the workshop to be equipped with a variety of cramps. They are used for gluing up pieces for final assembly and as an extra pair of hands (or more) to hold irregular or large pieces of work. Good quality bar cramps are T-sectioned for strength and are expensive, but it will be clear once the craftsman has used them just how important these are to glue-jointed structures. It should be stressed, however, that work must be protected from the cramp's jaws, by using a piece of softwood between them and the surfaces of the project. G-cramps are used for holding smaller pieces together and come in a variety of sizes.

The one time I had taken a bong in Salamanca I found myself in a version of the film. Jack Cardiff[79] gave me a pep-talk: "Don't worry about your skin. It's amazing what I can do. It's going to be great."

I was on set in full flying gear, moustached à la David Niven, my darling machine all set up in front of me:

SEBASTIAN: Anyone can fly.
NAPPER: Why should I believe you?
SEBASTIAN: You *know*, if I can do it, you'll do it so much more easily, and better.
NAPPER: *Mulling over what Sebastian says.* Yes, you're right.
ELENA: (as Kim Hunter[80]): You can do it, Matt.
Napper nods at her and sits on the machine. It takes a moment for the machine to register his presence, then whoosh. Elena screams and turns her face into Sebastian's chest. He takes her face in his hands.
SEBASTIAN: These things happen in war.
ELENA: *Looking into Sebastian's eyes.* Yes.

[79] Cinematographer and director. Photographed *A Matter of Life and Death*
[80] She plays David Niven's love interest, June

Yes. Oh, Sebastian. I don't know what I'd do if I lost you, too.

She sounded genuinely surprised to hear from me.

"You home?"

"Yes, well, I know what you mean, but I don't think of it as home any more."

"But you're here."

"Yes. I was wondering whether you'd like to come out."

"That'd be great," she said. "I don't get out much, you know, with the kids."

There was no doorbell or knocker so I rattled the letter-box. The door opened and she stood in the hallway with the light behind her so that she was a silhouette with a glowing edge.

"See you later!" she called as she closed the door. "Hi! Great to see you."

I spent my whole childhood hardly able to speak to her because I was too nervous, and now she was in the front seat of my van, inches away, and it felt utterly right.

"Where are we going?" she said.

"No idea. Where do people go round here, now?"

"Let's just drive somewhere, shall we?"

We stopped at the Halfway on the coast road. I could hardly believe her beauty when she sat opposite me. She had such a fresh complexion, still, her eyes bright and her mouth curling at each corner. It was such a positive face. **Looking into Sebastian's eyes. Yes. Yes. Oh, Sebastian. I don't know what I'd do if I lost you, too.** At that moment, I felt that I could be happy.

If the craftsman is going to make a number of frames, mitre cramps are a wise addition to workshop equipment. They can hold the members of a frame perfectly – as long as the mitres have been cut true – allowing fixing to be carried out comfortably. Although a mitred joint is relatively easy to cut, it looks appalling if cut inaccurately. However, as with all good cramps, it is possible to 'pull up' minor discrepancies in a joint's cut, which will be hidden by the pressure of the cramps and a solid, permanent fix.

"It's good to see you," she said.

"It's good to see you, too." I put the gift on the table between us and pushed it towards her. "I've brought you a little something."

"What for?"

"You know. Old times. Haven't seen you for a long time. That kind of thing."

She untied the ribbon. "You've wrapped it beautifully." She folded back the paper to reveal the box. "Oh my god, it's gorgeous!"

I was pleased with it, too, the timber expressing the form of the box crisply. I had used decorative through-dovetails in a form of quiet ostentation.

"It's so lovely," she said. "Thank you."

"Have a look inside."

She flipped the bronze catch – I was using bronze in everything now – and lifted the lid.

"Did you make this, too?"

"That too."

"Wow! I've never had one."

She lifted the Love Spoon[81] over the lid and closed the box. I had carved it from a single piece of lime, which not only lends itself well to the task but a species which is especially sensual, its grain so compliant with one's strokes.

"That's so thoughtful," she said. "I've never had anything like this before. No one's ever made anything for me."

"Good," I said, "I'm glad."

"What do all these things mean, then?" She turned it over in her hands, touching the parts carefully.

"Well, they can mean a variety of things."

"These things," she said, touching the spheres in the cage.

"They can represent the number of children you have or will have, or they can be you and your partner or the seeds of life." I adjusted my jeans.

---

[81] A great deal of nonsense has been written about Love Spoons. Although not exclusive to Wales, they are primarily a token of love from a man to a woman, incorporating symbols which are often specific to the man who has carved it. As such, they are an example of folk art which existed at a time when a man's craft skills were appreciated

"Oh, that's so clever. It's such a lovely thing. I'll treasure it," she said, reaching across the table and putting her hand upon mine. The electricity shocked through me. **I don't know what I'd do if I lost you.**

Perhaps I could be. Perhaps she could be. Perhaps we could be.

Chapter Eleven

When I opened my eyes I was looking up at a flat expanse of ceiling so large that I felt I had woken on the other side of life. That I was in hospital only became clear when I turned my head and saw the sign ONLY TWO VISITORS PER PATIENT. Then the waffle blanket on my chest and the large frame over my midriff also alerted my senses. And looking out of the window was Conductor 71,[82] the French fop responsible for the dead, his frock-coat and stockings perfectly aligned.

"Ah, you're awake!"

"What are you doing here? This isn't *your* film," I said.

"What? What film? What's that, my love?"

Then the nurse came into focus.

"I thought you were someone else," I said.

"I'm Sally," she said. "You're in hospital."

"Hospital?"

"Got it in one, love. I'm just going off now but I'll see you tomorrow."

She was leaning over me and I closed my eyes, the effects of her long shift on her body and perfume following me into another world. I walked through the door and joined the queue behind Bull, Dog, Ev and Napper.

"Sign here, please," the nurse instructed.

The boys were suddenly behaving well, their school ties tight to their necks and their shoes polished.

"They're not usually like this," I wanted to say. "They're horrible. All of them."

The nurse smiled at each of them and waved her arm to the right to direct them.

"Name?" she said to me.

"Tim."

She looked at the register in front of her. "I'm sorry, there's no Tim here. Perhaps you've come to the wrong place."

[82] Played by Marius Goring in the film *A Matter of Life and Death*

"But you let them in," I protested.

"We were expecting them."

I woke to the ceiling vast above my head again.

Elena visits me, wearing her white gown and talking to me softly with her arms outstretched – "Tim, Tim" – but there is something peculiar about my reaction. I sense my heart pounding and my breath quickening, yet the electricity which usually buzzes around the centre of my being is replaced by a disconnection. She is calling and calling. Then she changes into Conductor 71.

CONDUCTOR: **What do you think you are doing here?**

TIM: **Making plans.**

CONDUCTOR: **The dead do not make plans, monsieur.**

TIM: **I am planning to kill.**

CONDUCTOR: *Flicking his handkerchief.* **You are wicked. You must come with me this instant.**

TIM: **But I have plans. My time is just beginning.**

CONDUCTOR: **Pa! We shall see about this.** *He changes into a* **Corvus corax**[83] *and* **"kaws"** *at Tim from the foot of the bed.*

I woke screaming and the nurse rushed in.

"I was dreaming."

"We heard you right down the ward," she said. "Dreams don't hurt."

I pointed to where my notes hung. "There was a raven on my bed."

The nurse made a show of looking all around and under the bed. "Well it's not here now, Tim."

The way she said "Tim" struck me, a name too small to accommodate my future. One only had to pronounce the initial phoneme with one's voice for it to become "Dim". Bull, Dog, Ev

---

[83] Raven

69

and Napper had treated me as such even though their individual selves were dim, as in existing with an absence of light. My plans were to furnish their final light.

I watched the clouds passing across the windows' squares until I was able to stand and look over the grounds where *Pica pica* and *Corvus frugilegus*[84] made a cacophony in a copper beech. *Ardea cinerea*[85] lurked by the pond. I used the book Elena had brought me to read about them, even though I already knew what I needed. The book, even then, was somewhat disappointing. The illustrations – watercolours – were quite poor: the nest, the egg and, worst of all, the monochromatic bird in the top left hand corner, one up the rung from appalling. This was publishing on the cheap. What I'd always wanted was a field guide merely for the area in which I lived. The pages on sea birds such as *Rissa tridactyla, Fulmarus glacialis, Alca torda* and *Uria aalge*[86] were a complete waste. The only coast I'd seen was the slick of mud in Newport[87] when the river was on the ebb or the view from Twmbarlwm.[88] The closest I got to the *blue* sea was the travel programmes on television.

I considered suicide, of course. It was rather fleeting but long enough to evaluate methods within my immediate clinical context. In fact there was a dearth of possibilities open to me. I could try to execute the deed with a piece of hospital cutlery which even found the Rizla-thin hospital ham a trial, or I could throw myself from the window. The former was appallingly vulgar and quickly discounted as laborious, painful and lacking in poise; the latter had too great a risk of failure, leaving me alive yet too badly injured to finish myself off, unlike Peter Carter bailing out of his stricken bomber without his parachute only to regain consciousness with nothing more than a missing boot. Besides, I had so very much to look forward to:

[84] Rook
[85] Grey Heron
[86] Kittiwake, Fulmar, Razorbill and Guillemot
[87] Situated on the river Usk's slimy slide into the sea. The third largest town in Wales
[88] A hill about eight miles north of Newport, on the summit of which is an iron-age hill fort

- more hospital food (I liked the ham sandwiches of sliced white bread)
- more visits from junior doctors who came to see what a eunuch looked like
- the birds out the window
- the clouds building and breaking
- Bull's, Dog's, Ev's and Napper's faces as I imagined their lights going out
- the consultations with the psychologist
- the police interviews
- Elena.

Who had ever heard of such a thing as a hospital pond? There is no doubt that it helped me to recover, however, and to gain some clarity on my situation. It was like looking at a microcosm: the butcher, the baker, the candlestick maker going about their business: *Corvus frugilegus* enjoying a riotous chorus, *Pica pica* burgling when no one was looking, and *Ardea cinerea* like a detective hunched in a raincoat. *Buteo buteo* occasionally graced the community with its presence like a passing dignitary. The pond provided at least one strawberry moment during my time there and was a diversion from the boys I imagined having the strength to hurt over and over again. Killing them formulated itself as my life's work as I watched the clouds gather and break outside the window. I was delighted to have found my purpose in life so early on. I discovered later that some people never find a purpose in life but stumble from one thing to another, having mid-life crises and traumatic stock-takes of their lives. I was fortunate. And once my destiny had been fulfilled I would be able to rest. The time scale was integral to my purpose: rushing would be entirely detrimental.

Elena also brought me a set of sketching pencils in a tin and a spiral bound sketchbook. I drew:
- the water jug
- the hill framed by the window
- the chair at the side of the bed
- the sink

- an apple with light coming from the left and an apple with light coming from the right. I blended each lead into the next as carefully as I could to represent the gradation from dark tones to light. The psychologist found these interesting.

"Tell me, Tim, what are these?" she said, turning the pad around on the desk and pushing it towards me.

"Apples."

"I see."

"This one's drawn with the lamp coming from the left, this one's with the lamp coming from the right."

"Ah. I thought they were something else."

"I thought it was obvious."

"Well, no. Considering what has happened to you, I thought they were your testes."

That was a lemon moment, the first indication that whatever I did, or was going to do, would be interpreted by other people differently to how I intended. I wondered what she would think of my plans. No doubt she would take a Freudian paradigm and extrapolate something outlandish and give it a name that would label me as something-or-other. I was merely a teenage boy who had had his balls removed; there was nothing more to it than that. And I was going to get my own back. Full stop. No one would have argued with that.

Chapter Twelve

Multi-planes are similar to combination planes but can perform a number of extra tasks because of their extra cutters: grooves, housing, rebates, tongue and grooves, beads, ovolo mouldings, flutes and reeds.

As well-made as they were, my darling's wings of *Acer pseudoplatanus* were too flat and lacking in definition, and as soon as I became dissatisfied with them I worked on their re-design feverishly, going through a pad of paper developing ideas. The thin cross-sections of timber were fine but represented a single feather that ran the length of the wing, akin to a hand-fan. The new design actually recreated a bird's wing more closely: primaries, secondaries, greater primary coverts, greater coverts, alula, median primary coverts, lesser primary coverts, marginal coverts, lesser coverts, median coverts, axillaries. Instead of using *Acer pseudoplatanus* throughout, however, I wanted to blend the 'feathers' from the leading edge to the primaries in gradually lightening species. There would also be an eighth of an inch step from one set to the next to create the effect of layering. That there were four main layers also meant a return to the initial selection of timbers in the main structure, namely *Fraximus excelsior, Swietenia macrophylla, Carya illinoensis* and *Dalbergia frutescens*.

It was odd that I had not realised that I should have found the answer to the problem of the wings much earlier, considering my interest in and knowledge of birds. I was fortunate to find, also, the carcass of a *Buteo buteo*, and so used it as a model. The challenge was to design wings which successfully represented the feathers without losing myself in unnecessary intricacy. I made four pairs before I arrived at what I expected to be the final version.

Grooves are most often planed with the grain. They can be cut in end grain but the craftsman must be careful of splitting the edge at the end of the pass. It is best to cut out the waste at

the end of the cut with a saw and chisel before carrying out the task with the plane.

"So why'd you come back this time?" Elena asked.

"Timber for my furniture."

"Oh, right."

"Yes. I go to great lengths to get what I want for my designs."

"Doesn't that make it expensive?"

"Extremely."

"It's not the kind of stuff you'd buy in Howells's[89] then?"

"No."

"Sounds as if you make a fair bit of money."

"Enough to keep me comfortable, that's all. I only make a few pieces a year. The clients are the people with money."

"What timber you after here?"

"*Fagus sylvatica*," I said. "That's European Beech but I wanted it from Wales."

"What are you making?"

"It's a project I've been working on for some time. Something for me. I keep adding to it and changing it."

"Must be lovely. What is it, exactly?"

I hesitated. "A chair. It's getting there." **You are wicked,** the Conductor interrupted.

What was I saying? It was hardly a chair. It was a thing of beauty. Yes, Dog had sat on it but chair was a misnomer. It was closer to the Electric Chair than a chair on which one might relax and eat and talk and laugh and enjoy the everyday sensations of being alive. But it was far swifter and more elegant than the crudeness of electric currents passing through a body until dead.[90]

Elena took a sip from her glass of beer and I looked over her shoulder. **You are wicked.**

"How are you, you know, now?"

"Well, I'm never going to be a dad, of course." But she knew that.

"You can still be a dad," she said.

---

[89] Department store in Cardiff, south Wales

[90] The first Electric Chair was made of oak. Another reason to omit it from my design

"How do you work that out?"

"It's not just about being able to father a child."

"I've never thought about it any other way."

"That's daft," she said. "You can still be a dad."

I don't know what I'd do if I lost you.

I did not know what it is like to have sex with a woman. And since the boys had ruined me I hadn't even been able to masturbate.

"You remember Dog and Bull?"

"I never liked them."

"They're both dead."

"What!"

"Murdered. Really odd, the police say. About a year apart."

"Rubbed up someone the wrong way, did they?"

Elena shrugged.

"What happened?"

"Bull had a nail in his head, though he had so much alcohol in his blood they reckon he didn't feel anything, and Dog was stabbed several times. The police think they're linked."

"Nail!" **You are wicked.**

"That's what they reckon. They're not making everything public, they said."

"I wonder why." **You are wicked.**

"And he left something behind. One copper said on the telly that he'd never seen anything like it in thirty years in the force."

"God!"

"You didn't like them, did you?"

"They weren't the shiniest apples in the barrel."

There was a pause.

Housings are grooves cut across the grain. The multi-plane must be guided by a temporary fence clamped to the timber.

The painting to which I felt most affinity was *The Martyrdom of Saint Sebastian*[91] by the brothers Piero and Antonio del Pollaiuolo. Sebastian is high on a tree trunk with his hands tied behind his back, his head

[91] In the National Gallery, London. Completed in about 1475

raised heavenwards, and six men firing up at him. They are using simple machines – bow and crossbow. The latter reminded me that even something which has been designed for killing can still fail if the person using it does not possess the skills necessary for its success. I had killed two men but had failed to prove myself to myself.

To see the painting in the flesh, so to speak, was beyond doubt a strawberry-plus moment. The reproductions I had seen in no way prepared me for the huge image, physically upon the wall and emotionally in its effect upon me. But it was not just the image that affected me – the pyramid-like composition of the six men around the bole, the depth to which the arrows had penetrated Sebastian's flesh, his barely concealed genitalia which immediately recalled the moment which had brought me to this point – it was what was never revealed in the reference books: the frame. It was as worthy of attention as the image itself, its craftsmanship completely unsung, designed in architecturally beautiful proportions like a portico: plinths supporting columns swagged with acanthus leaves, gryphons, eagles and the torsos of winged cherubs, all gessoed and burnished with gold leaf. 'Frame' was inappropriate for such a wonderful object. After seeing it I never considered the painting as separate from the craftsmanship which framed it. To me they depended upon each other in a sublime state of symbiosis.

To cut a rebate, the multi-plane is set up as if to cut a groove but the fence is adjusted so that the cutter is brought to the edge of the piece of work. Wider rebates can be cut by cutting one blade width at a time.

"So would you ever come back?" Elena asked.

"I'm back now."

"To live, I mean."

"It's still home but I think it's a place that exists for me in memory, that's all."

"What's it like where you live?"

"Similar to here, I suppose, as far as the landscape is concerned, but I live near a city on the north coast. It's ugly, actually, but the village is lovely. So are the food and the cafés. Everyone goes to the cafés."

"I went to the Costa Brava when I was a kid," she said. "The only time I've been abroad. I'd like to travel but, you know, can't do much with the kids and stuff."

"Travel's good."

"You've done a bit, have you?"

"Yes, it's been good. But it's strange how I keep being drawn back here, even though I don't want to live here."

"Even this is strange to me," Elena said, looking around us.

I wanted to say, *Come and stay with me. Free holiday. You'd like it. The beach is fantastic and the shops and atmosphere are wonderful. You can sit in cafés all day and watch the world go by. I'll work and we can eat together in the evening and cwtch[92] in bed until we fall asleep.*

She might have been expecting me to offer but that would have interfered with my reason for existence ever since waking in the hospital. There was no one with whom I could share what I had in mind. Mine was a solitary pleasure, a singular existence, a personal necessity. I looked at her across the table and thought how extraordinary it was that she still caused me to ignite. She was completely ignorant about what she did to me. Her beauty played with my intellectual freedom. It was difficult to resist offering her the world as I knew it, telling her what I was really doing there, wanting to share it. And this dreadful pub, with its faux antiquity, was exotic to her. She was stuck.

"It's nice, isn't it?" she said.

I could have cried. "I can't remember the last time I was in a pub," I said, by way of deflecting saying anything detrimental about the place.

"Nor me," she said.

My heart sank. I could have died for her, taken her place on the stairway to heaven and traded in my life to extend hers, so that she could see and do wonderful things instead of living her narrow monotonous existence.

The tongue cutter has an integral depth stop, so doing away with the need for a depth adjuster on the multi-plane itself.

---

[92] A dialect word from south Wales meaning to cuddle

The guide fence is set to centre the tongue on the edge of the timber and the groove cutter is set to match the tongue after it has been planed.

When I re-lived the evening I could hardly believe that I had described my darling as a common chair. Even by that time it was an exquisite piece, its proportions balanced and forthright. Even then I was proud of it. Looking at it under the spots back home (by which I mean at Casa Arbol), I realised all too slowly, how similar in concept it had become to the chair awarded to the Welsh poets.[93] The men who would be chaired by my piece would momentarily be the centre of attention before they were dispatched by the weight of their selves. The chair would allow them to achieve the greatness they would never otherwise achieve. It recognised them for a moment in the weight of their current self, balanced that against the design I had created, and killed them. Oh how beautiful it would be when it worked as I had intended. *Made to make your eyes water.* A strawberry moment as intense as the sun, more intense, even, than that sun which had taken my breath away in Salamanca the evening Stacey Leibnitz said she was in love with me.

It wasn't possible physically or emotionally. I had determined to devote my life to meeting those who had changed my life and Stacey strengthened my resolve to see it through. As it was, we spent a great deal of time together. It was she who took me into Salamanca's cathedrals first, the sudden drop in temperature unsettling as I walked from the first into the older second building. But I never attended services there. The closest I got to a ceremony was the Easter celebrations, the virgins of the city robed in white and carrying the Mother of God on their shoulders, with her arms outspread and flowers at her feet. Men dressed in white or black robes with pointed hoods like the Ku Klux Klan followed. It was quite different from the marching bands with kazoos I had witnessed at home.

---

[93] The chairing ceremony at the National Eisteddfod of Wales. A bardic chair is designed for each eisteddfod and awarded to the poet who wins the competition for a poem written in strict metre. The chairs are highly prized. They are usually large, with a high back like a throne

Stacey kissed me in Café Jazz. She had got closer and closer the more she drank. She sat opposite me at first, then moved to the side of the table, her toes and knees against mine. I didn't discourage her and when we kissed it set off something inside me, but the electricity didn't reach my penis. Egon Schiele's *Self-Portrait as St. Sebastian*[94] – a stunning poster in Indian ink and gouache – expresses how I felt when I received Stacey's kisses and could not return them, hands raised and open towards her, each arrow's barbs ready to fix in the flesh never to be pulled out, like the hook in the *perca fluviatilis* with which I had strung out its guts. The roughness of Schiele's arrows are quite unlike Gerrit van Honthorst's in his painting *Saint Sebastian*,[95] which are crisp and straight, piercing well-fed and folded flesh, though there are only four of them. One of them appears to pierce the heart, however. I wondered what it would be like to feel Stacey's breasts against my cheeks but told her I was in love with someone back home, even though my darling competed to push Elena out.

The special fence for cutting beads automatically positions the cutter to create the moulding just above the tongue. The bead can be cut further from the edge by using the multi-plane's standard fence.

---

[94] (26 3/8" x 19 3/4"), 1914–15, Historisches Museum der Stadt Wien, Vienna
[95] (39 3/4" x 46 1/16") about 1623, The National Gallery, London

Chapter Thirteen

Stacey was wearing a short skirt that first night. Her legs were smooth and brown and made me aware of my own pale skin. When she sat on the stool I could see the mystery of her thighs, hinting at something to discover. She was well made and well proportioned, and I liked her knees' definite lines. I saw them in wood: some kind of knuckle joint, perhaps, in mahogany, then rubbed down through the sandpaper grades from coarse to very fine. Hours and hours on the astonishing smoothness of her thighs. I would get to know her lines when she came to see me after Jesús's death.

There was something missing. She had it but I didn't. It couldn't be made. It existed for Elena but not for Stacey. And as skilful as I am, it's something I couldn't make.

What is the matter with you? the Conductor wanted to know. **Are you not a man with blood in your veins? What kind of wickedness is this, that you push away a beautiful woman?**

"There's something missing."

But monsieur, she has everything, no? He waved his cane at me.

"She does, I don't."

You have a beating heart, monsieur, which is more than I have!

"There is no electricity."

I do not understand, he said, banging his cane on the floor.

Stacey butted in: "What did you say? You talking to yourself?"

"Was I?"

"You know what they say, first sign of madness."

A comment like that merely added to whatever it was that kept the electricity switched off.

I have no idea where the word came from but a bird in an egg is a *yukka*. An egg was *yukka-ed*. Blood would trickle out of the holes pierced in the shell as an indication that it was too late to augment one's collection with this particular jewel: it was a trinket now. Blowing an egg like this would result in it smashing in one's hands. *Yukka*, to my ears, sounded remarkably close to eunuch, the final syllable catching in my throat – [nʌk]– phonetically encapsulating my essence, my lack of power, my lack of worth. YOU-NUCK. A second person travesty.

An ovolo moulding is cut just like a rebate.

I enjoyed drawing in the hospital because it used up whole chunks of time in intense concentration, which would be good practice for my project. I drew the hill first, the window frame making it easier to measure its presence in the space it occupied. I had always been good at drawing but I actually credit this period with my ability to draw in a sustained manner. I learned to measure, not precisely in the design sense, but in my ability to allow an object or thing to be expressed accurately through its proportions. The hill existed as a set of proportions within the boundaries of the window and the jug was a set of proportions which divided itself in a number of ways. It had a solid pose, proportion and form and presented itself in the shape of a woman, a shape which was becoming increasingly abstract to me. I once saw, quite accidentally, Elena in her underwear when the door to the girls' changing room was open. She was wearing a light blue bra and pants. Now, even the time I spent masturbating over her that night was a memory.

I touched myself carefully under the frame: my penis had shrunk back like the snout of a tortoise in its shell, and that odd space my testes once occupied was covered with a dressing. I was afraid to look. There was much I would have to get accustomed to.

I tried to coax my penis to react to my finger tips, encouraging the shaft to appear from somewhere out of sight, by thinking of Elena in her underwear again, but to no avail. Even when she visited and her presence was fresh, still nothing happened. The fuse had been blown.

Flutes are cut like beads. Use the standard fence and depth gauge.

There was something enormously satisfying about the chair at the side of the bed and my first achievement was to sit in it.

"We'll have you out of bed for an hour today," the nurse said.

I nearly passed out when I had first been propped up so the thought of leaving the safety of the bed at all was disturbing. A nurse stood either side of me and held me standing for a moment before easing me onto the seat. I saw the breasts of one of the nurses when her uniform gaped as she stood in front of me. They were lovely breasts but the interest that would have flickered in my penis did not register. The chair, however, was a great comfort. They put a waffle blanket over me and I enjoyed the sensation of resting my forearms upon the arms of the chair and cupping their scroll in the palms of my hands. It gave me strength because the chair's legs were in line with the frame upon which my whole being rested. I was part of the floor and the floor was connected to the walls and the ceiling and these were connected to the foundations deep beneath me. It was a new experience. Apart from the task I was setting myself, it was all I had.

Reed cutters create parallel beads all at once. The plane is set up as if for a flute or bead.

It was the Conductor's flick of the wrist, so practised and so aristocratic, which made me say, "Tell me, monsieur, how *did* you die?"

Mon Dieu! Is there no end to your insolence? Monsieur, you have *no manners*.

"I see, you don't want to talk about it."

Monsieur, please!

"You did something wrong."

Enough, monsieur! He put his hand to his neck then turned his back on me, the silk folds of his coat shimmering. His shoulders shook and he made the noises a child makes when trying to stifle the sounds of crying.

"Is the guillotine as terrible as they say?"

Monsieur!

"For me it lacks finesse. It's industrial. One size fits all. My work, on the other hand, considers each individual's presence then marries them in an instant of grace."

Monsieur, you must stop.

Chapter Fourteen

Ev had always been big. I had been right through school with him, and even made a den with him once when friendships were several. His hair had always been the same style, which was no style, with a straight fringe and no parting. It looked the same, wet or dry.

The first Physical Education lesson in which we played rugby, he had been pulled out of the line to play prop forward and remained in that position for the duration of his school career. What he lacked in athleticism he made up for in strength and what appeared to be an inability to feel pain. The opposition hit him and crumpled, and when he had the ball he steam-rollered down the field, knowing that he would be stopped by sheer numbers, only. I hung around on the wing waiting for the ball to come to me, hoping that I wouldn't be tackled in case I snapped.

After spending so much time perfecting the wings I felt that Ev would be flown to the next world, or wherever he was going. He deserved to go to that place for which the only semblance of preparation is three hours in skin-blistering heat on a Spanish beach. I had learned a great deal from my experiences with Bull and Dog, so expected much more. Ev was orange, too, so I expected his death to be good at least. It was worse than either previous experience and as a result I nearly quit, which would have been a tragedy indeed, after all these years of study and practice, the death performed again and again on storyboards pinned to the walls behind my eyes.

A nail in the head would have been an exciting death for the village. No one had been killed there in all the time I had lived there. The local newspaper's focus was five miles away in Newport, a city whose claim to fame was the Chartists.[96] To discover a corpse with a six-inch

[96] The Chartists fought for social and political reform, demanding universal suffrage for men over 21; electoral districts of equal size; voting by secret ballot; an end to the need for property to become an MP; pay for MPs; annual election of Parliament. There was a riot in Newport and twenty Chartists were killed by troops hiding in the Westgate Hotel

nail in its head would have made a local police officer's day: "At last!" I could hear him say, something to investigate rather than a theft from a garden shed. To discover another body with circumstantial similarities would have made him feel out of his depth.

Elena put me off. I was not actually back for any species of timber but was there to kill Ev. I had never considered the police before then. All my preparations had been for killing only, and to learn from her that the police had made a connection between the deaths – different though they were – was not a surprise. I had left something behind for each of them and had taken something also. Elena had not mentioned that, perhaps because the police had not released the information to the *South Wales Argus*. I kept what I had taken in my grandfather's box. I was not afraid of being caught but I was afraid of being prevented from my life's work. To complete my plans partially would have been death to me. The risk was too great so all I did was walk along the canal where I met the boy I had been and the man I had become at various points: where I caught fish, where I found nests. I returned to Casa Arbol without having seen Ev. There was no rush and the longer I left it the better. I would visit again but would leave my darling behind and in the meantime I began to design my coffin.

The dovetail joint is so versatile. It is used in the construction of drawers and that of log cabins. The more one tries to pull apart a dovetail joint the stronger it is. The joint is attractive, too, and can be enhanced by joining two differently coloured timbers.

Jesús showed me how to cut a dovetail joint without even marking out the timber. He had been cutting such joints for so long that the ratio was ingrained in his being, and when he cut out for the tail the fit was superb. Then he showed me again, this time using the dovetail template and a pin-sharp pencil. When he had cut the tail he placed it on the female piece and marked it with the point of the pencil tight against the tail.

"Some people use a hacksaw blade because it's fine but the mark made by a hard-leaded pencil is finer," he said.

Marking accurately did not ensure a good joint, however, because the cut had to be executed accurately. Being able to control the tool in the hand – whatever it might be – was one of the most important skills of all. The tool had to do whatever was required of it. I knew what it should do and I knew what the result was meant to be, but these rarely coincided. A craftsman is a person whose skills mean that he makes few mistakes and when he does make one, he can get out of it. I made many mistakes and in the beginning I could not get out of them. But Jesús telling me to start again was admonishment enough.

"I made mistakes when I started," he said.

Before dinner that evening I asked him when he had started working with wood.

"I've loved being in a workshop ever since my father took me into my grandfather's coffin workshop. The smell was the first thing that hit me, then the colours and textures of the timbers all around. When I saw the tools, that was it. Most of my tools were his. They don't make them like this any more," he said, holding up a smoothing plane.[97] "So you must buy them whenever the opportunity arises."

What stayed with me were not just the tools – for which I have paid large amounts of money since – but the need for a hand-made coffin. I would have asked Jesús to make it if I had had the choice but as he would pre-decease me, I had to do it. The coffins most people settle for are made in factories and veneered. I wanted something solid – of course – and personal.

A coffin is merely a box. I had made many boxes by the time I came to make the coffin but I did not want to make anything as predictable as those which people recognised instantly. Firstly, I did not wish to follow the usual European form. I preferred the simplicity of an oblong. It also had to be constructed in a manner which made it clear *how* it was made, with dovetails at each corner. Other striking external and internal features were important to me. Looking at American caskets, I wondered how they had evolved into their present cumbersome and unwieldy design. The British design was recognisable by its austerity,

[97] A Norris No. 5 coffin-shaped plane with rosewood infill

whilst the Italian used the same shape but applied an ornate Catholic crucifix or machine-carved head of Christ on the side.

I went as far as writing:

I, Sebastiáno del Arbol, wish to be buried in the coffin I have made for my burial.

I wish to be dressed in my leather apron.

I wish my Estwing hammer to be placed in my right hand.

I wish my Disston saw to be placed in my left hand.

I wish a bag of three inch oval nails to be placed next to me.

I shall be prepared[98] for the next world.

Sebastiáno del Arbol

---

[98] With these items I could make a battened door into the next world

Chapter Fifteen

Any boy with the barest of rugby talent in Wales became a schoolboy international, so Ev was picked. The team beat all the home sides and the Head called Ev out in the assembly to present him with his cap. Ev lumbered out of his seat, a simulacrum of athleticism as far as I could tell, embarrassed and awkward in front of his peers. The Head praised him and said how we should all look forward to seeing him on our screens defeating the 'old enemy' in future years. It raised Ev's profile in the school.

Ev's face appeared regularly on the back pages of the paper after that. I wondered what went through his head when he saw himself grinning from the newsprint. I thought he looked even more moronic than he did in real life.

It is important to adopt a comfortable and purposeful stance when cutting joints. It is usual to stand with one's left foot forward, knee bent, and the right leg straight. (Reverse if you are left-handed.) Some craftsmen find that standing with one's feet apart is also a strong stance though it is easier to lose balance.

The craftsman must be flexible, however, since it is not always possible to cut in the same position in all situations, especially if working outside the workshop. Ultimately it is the handling of the tools which is most important. Being able to use them in different situations defines the craftsman's skill.

It was easy to track him down when it was his turn to meet my darling. He had made the transition to first-class rugby and was still making a splash in the back pages of the local press:

After his storming performance on Saturday, Evans's grasp of the number 1 jersey must be assured. The selectors witnessed his almost flawless demonstration of front-row skill in the set piece and in open play.

"I'm delighted with my game," said Evans. "I've been working hard on my fitness and now I'm reaping the rewards."

But it was his crucial try on the cusp of half-time that should guarantee his place in the Welsh squad. After a one-handed take he charged to the line like a bull, tacklers bouncing off him in a vain attempt at preventing the score.

It will be a crime if Evans does not get the nod this time.

And there he was, his features bulging out of the photograph, a bigger version of the boy he'd been, one of the next heroes of Welsh rugby.

Rasps and rifflers are used infrequently in the workshop unless you are carving. Rasps remove waste quickly because they cut with and against the grain. The rough surface is then smoothed with files of a similar shape. There are three types: bastard, second-cut and smooth, which can be purchased as flat and round. The most useful, however, is the half-round rasp.

It didn't please me that I would be depriving the national team of one of its props, an essential element in its power house, but it couldn't be helped. Ev was going to walk onto my pitch.

What I had in store for him wasn't at all appropriate for an international rugby player but entirely appropriate for a moron. My darling would take him in her arms, size him up as if he were an opponent, and surprise him in the purest of moves. Seeing him in that photograph made me doubt my intentions momentarily, for surely it wasn't right that he should deserve such love? The love with which I had designed each component, sharpened each of my tools, laboured for years. Then I reminded myself that he was one of *the* reasons for which this love had shown itself in glorious wood.

Wood files take off the rough surface created by the rasp. These are also described as having bastard, second-cut and smooth cuts, but are quite fine in comparison to rasps.

His moronic laugh is what I recognised first. The team had won. Friends and fans greeted players with a pat on the back or a shake of the hand when they came into the bar. Then I saw from where the laugh emanated. He looked almost respectable in his blazer but his shirt didn't button at the neck, so that the collar's wings splayed and his tie merely rested on his chest. What really took me aback was his lack of hair. The dry straw-coloured mess was gone. His head shone under the lights.

A Surform is a fairly recent development. It has a thin punched blade whose teeth all face forward. The wood shavings pass through the blade in a similar way to a cheese grater so that it does not clog the teeth. There are a variety of Surforms on the market but the flat file and round hollow file will be suitable for most purposes.

I was happier for him to meet my darling than I had been about Bull and Dog. I wasn't fooled by his ill-fitting clothes. He deliberately wore items which were too small to give a greater impression of size. He wasn't that big. If I could size him up so easily then my darling wouldn't be fooled. It would be a good marriage.

Rifflers are small files with a cutting head at each end, designed for working in the confined areas of a project. Wonderful accuracy can be achieved in the presentation of detail.

I suppose it was inevitable that once I had carved the wings, I would be tempted to decorate other components of my darling. The wings lifted her into another dimension, with the weights registering the mortals in order to transport them to a state of immortality. But I kept in mind the purity of expression I had set out to achieve and decoration was kept to a minimum. Rather than overloading my darling with an icing of pomposity, I looked for those places where decoration would *accent* the form. It meant that some of the pieces had to be re-made. Apart from the techniques of construction which had been used for generations, I became quite taken with the notion that she should have a kind of history, a language of previous generations.

Firstly, I wanted to do something about her feet.

I was sickened to learn that Ev was a carpenter. His name struck across the side of his van. How could *he* be a carpenter? How could he *know* wood? I needn't have worried.

I saw his work. He didn't *know* wood. There was no finesse involved. He forced things together when they didn't fit, filled gaps with glue and sawdust, hammered in screws to save time. It might as well have been hunks of meat with which he was working. It did present me with a way of meeting him, however.

I didn't want a generic claw and ball foot. I wanted to copy a real foot. *Falco tinnunculus* was too delicate, used to picking up very small mammals, *Accipiter nisus* was more ferocious but still rather small. *Falco peregrinus* had the strength and form to make it look as if the ball in its grasp would never be released.[99]

I visited the National Birds of Prey Centre and spent hours drawing the feet of a bird called Daedalus.[100] Then I replicated them in the workshop using a variety of gouges for the feet and a Japanese firmer outcannel gouge for the balls.

I eventually did have the good fortune to see *Falco peregrinus* in the wild. There are well-known sites in Wales which are inaccessible but I found one that wasn't well-known yet quite accessible. I parked my van from which it was easy to watch the male and female stooping near the quarry where they nested. They played with the *Columba oenas*[101] they killed, dropping it through the air to be caught by the

---

[99] Claw and ball feet were frequently used to decorate chairs, especially mahogany, produced in many workshops between 1755 and 1800. There are patterns in Chippendale's book

[100] Icarus would have been entirely inappropriate

[101] Stock Dove

mate, or let it go, injured but still able to fly, for their young to catch again.

It was only when I began to imitate the cello's scroll for the arms that I came to realise what a pleasing element it was going to be. Viewed from the side elevation it had the swirl of a snail shell, in the hand it had the finger-friendly fluting. It would work against the need for the arm to fall away, then spiral forward like a wave breaking, full of latent grace and power. When finished, the scrolls would take away my darling's lover's attention from what she was about to do for me. They were the one element encapsulating what would happen: a sudden stop, a consideration of an upward movement, a falling and spiral into the centre of the self.

I was surprised at how enthusiastic Ev was when he first saw my darling.

"Bloody hell, that's something else," he said, walking straight to her and placing his hand on a scrolled arm.

"You like it," I said.

"It's amazing. It's like a throne." He walked around her. "Yeah, just like a throne. Totally impractical but good enough to sit on for a short while."

I thought that was quite perceptive of him. But as for impractical, he was wrong.

"It's for the Eisteddfod or something, is it?"

I didn't really know how to answer.

"It's far too elaborate for a poet," I said. "It's a commission from a demanding client."

"So what's all this stuff about?" He pointed to the cupboard doors between the front legs. He stroked the wings.

I had my left hand in my pocket turning over what I had brought for him.

"This is fancy, en it?" He was examining her. "Bit too bloody fussy, I reckon." He *really* didn't know wood. "All right if..." he said, gesturing.

"Please," I said.

92

He cupped the scroll of each arm in his hands and began to ease himself onto the *Ulmus procera* seat. His left hand slipped, his weight shifted and he stumbled, falling to one side and causing my darling to shudder. She reacted by staggering her surprises rather than presenting them simultaneously. Ev's face clenched in a rictus of disbelief.

I had worked so hard for this terrible moment. I had tested her again and again. Ev had slipped and made a mess of things. Once a moron, always a moron.

Chapter Sixteen

I hadn't paid it much attention other than to recognise it as a broken Windsor chair. It wasn't an early one but a fair example of the nineteenth century.

"It was in my grandfather's workshop," Jesús said. "I remember him sitting in that of an evening."

"Why don't you fix it?"[102]

"One day," he said.

The next day I asked him if I could do it. He looked puzzled. "If you want."

"Yes, I'd like to."

So that was it. I'd always liked Windsor chairs. They were, to borrow Jesús's expression, honest. They had legs and a back and arms you could *feel* supporting you. This one had a broken arm support, a split seat and back legs that had been reduced in height so the whole chair stood at the wrong angle. Perhaps Jesús's grandfather had wanted to sit back rather than upright, quite befitting a man who spent his days making boxes for people in permanent repose. This was a chair in which a craftsman had relaxed.

Today glue tends to be stronger than the wood fibres themselves. Early glues were prone to disintegration because of moisture, which allowed joints to loosen. Much of today's restoration is due to this.

Stacey Leibnitz kept in touch. She hadn't let go. The fact that she had fallen in love with a man with no balls and no electricity,[103] was admirable. I always believed that my aura, or whatever you would like to call it – that particular expression of the self of which we're not conscious – sent out a signal which said I was a useless, sexless man. Thinking about it now I wonder whether there was something lacking

---

[102] Jesús would have thought 'restore' pretentious. "Restoration is for antique dealers," he once said, peremptorily. Another time he said, "It's second-hand furniture, that's all."

[103] It is not the correct word, I know, but the closest I can find

in Stacey, or some kind of hole in her self which my self fitted. She came to stay at Casa Arbol.

"I'm glad you're happy," she said.

I smiled at her but was injured by "happy". How could she know?

"I needed to see you like this," she said.

"Like what?"

"You are in love."

"What do you mean?"

"You are in love with what you are doing," she said.

I was glad she was pleased to think this was true but it has always irritated me when people have declared with such conviction that my behaviour was such-and-such. Everyone, it seemed, was a psychologist. I would, at that particular point in time, only be happy when I had killed beautifully.

Her visit made me realise however, that I was in love: the love I had had for Elena was now adult. There was no doubt that Stacey was beautiful, and I presume it was this beauty which made me recognize, again, Elena as fundamental to what I was doing. What was it that she had said? *It's not just about being able to father a child. You can still be a dad.* I would be able to pass on my skills to a son or a daughter.

The legs came out easily because of the condition of the whole chair. Then I was able to turn over the seat. I mixed cascamite,[104] glued the split and sash-cramped the seat together. Next were the butterfly keys.[105] I cut four. Then I placed the waist of each on the split itself and drew around them. I cut out the housing with a one inch chisel and ensured the depth was consistent. I glued each key in position. When the seat had dried, I planed the keys level with the seat base and released the clamps.

---

[104] A waterproof powdered resin wood glue. It is mixed with water to the consistency of cream

[105] Each key looks like a butterfly. It is a mirrored dovetail. I could have used softwood because the keys would not be seen, but I preferred to use the *Ulmus procera* from which the seat was carved

Jesús came in when I was mixing the stain for the butterfly keys.

"Leave it as it is," he said.

I must have looked surprised because he repeated himself.

"Leave it. It will be part of its life, its scars and history."

"You sure?"

"Sure. Leave it all. I want to be able to see what you've done."

The clash of opposites – Ev, for example, with my darling, a moron and an angel – was constant in Spain. Salamanca was an astonishing place to live, my days and nights at Café Jazz off the Plaza Mayor with Stacey were full of wonder, but I preferred the wild, green, northern world of Asturias, where there were wolves and bears in the mountains. No one would try and pass off Gijón as beautiful,[106] apart from the locals who didn't know any different.

It took some time to be inured to the sight of an old woman with a huge growth on her head, begging outside church, as women in leather and fur jackets brushed past, and butcher shops next door to brothels disguised as clubs. The older part of the town around the port – the Cimadevilla – was most interesting. The further you went up the streets, the fewer lights there seemed to be. *La Frontera* had a sign behind the bar in English: PEOPLE WITH GUNS WILL NOT BE SERVED.

The arm support was snapped, part of it sticking out of the seat. I drilled this out from beneath.

To re-form the support I joined it to another piece of *Fagus sylvatica,* then shaped it. I planed the broken face to an angle and positioned it on a squared piece of *Fagus sylvatica* and transferred that angle with a pencil. I cut this line and planed it so that it fitted the support. Then I glued and cramped them.

When dry, I put the support in a vice and shaped the new piece to match the tapered support of the other arm with a spokeshave. Then I smoothed with sandpaper and continued until it matched the height of the opposite arm.

---

[106] I couldn't help but think of it in similar terms to Dylan Thomas's Swansea, an "ugly lovely town"

I cut off the waste protruding below the seat and cut a narrow wedge from the bottom of the support. I cut a wedge to fit from the same species, glued it and hammered it into the slot. Finally, when the glue had dried, I cut the support flush with a paring chisel, and enjoyed the end-grain's fine shaving peeling over the cutting edge.

Monsieur, you are not fit to sit on such a chair.

"What do you know?"

He came to us in that chair and it was I who conducted him. This is he, he said, placing a sheet of paper in front of my face so that I could see the name Stanley James Raymond in a quilled hand.

"And?"

'And?' You are so rude!

"I am a craftsman."

You may be, he said, **but that is all you are.**

I brushed past him as I moved around the bench. "Isn't there somewhere you should be?"

I am here for you. He called over his shoulder as he swaggered out of the door, **One day, monsieur, one day.**

Because of the hard line created when it dries, animal glue can be cut with plane irons, and sanded. It can also be softened again with heat or water but this can affect the stability of the work carried out.

Modern glue guns heat cylinders of glue electrically. The gun is convenient and the glue sets in moments, which makes it excellent for mock-ups. Polyvinyl-Acetate (PVA) is non-toxic and is extremely popular with tradesmen and DIY-ers. It has an extraordinary shelf-life if kept at room temperature.

The back feet of Jesús's father's chair would have been much easier on a lathe but with no power tools in the workshop I shaped them with spokeshaves and gouges, checking their dimensions against the front feet with a set of callipers. I cut a 'tenon' which would go up inside the leg. I cut off each leg at the 'ankle' in order to disguise the joint for the new foot. I marked the centre of each leg with a centre finder.[107]

I drilled out the centre of the leg to a diameter which matched the round tenon I had shaped on each new foot. I glued the feet and used a sash cramp to secure.

I should have finished the repairs[108] by mixing stains to match the original colour, charged a rubber[109] with polish and finally waxed the whole chair, but I did as Jesús had asked. It came to me that was how I should regard my darling. Don't disguise the changes – which I was making – but incorporate them. Treat it as part of the design and making process. In that moment she went from something artificial and conceptualised, to something organic, something which would evolve. After all, her artificiality had not allowed her to love any of the subjects as she was meant to, so allowing her to change would enable her to adapt for them. This went against the philosophy with which I had approached the project when I first conceived it. But it is important to be open to new ways of doing things. She had started out as a sketch in a café. Now she was evolving to suit the changes that were occurring and which would enable me to ensure she was appropriate for her purpose.

---

[107] A centre finder allows you to find the centre of round stock of any size

[108] Some people would have said that I had restored rather than repaired. It was a chair with little value in the trade but was immensely valuable to me. Although I did not know Jesús's grandfather, it was enough for me that Jesús said he had been a fine craftsman. These repairs would last a long time but at some point in the future it is possible that another person would have to repair the chair again

[109] Used for applying French polish

Chapter Seventeen

The manner in which Ev died didn't really knock my confidence in my abilities but did send me to a place of darkness from which it took some time to emerge. I had dedicated myself to perfection, to creating something which demonstrated itself as such, and Ev's clumsiness – which I should have suspected from the moment I glimpsed his workmanship[110] – didn't recognise this. There were things over which I had no control, no matter what I did. For a while I wanted to give up. There was no point in continuing because the boys and the men they had become were spoiling it. What changed my mind was a day I spent at The National Gallery. I was on my way to see paintings of Saint Sebastian, again, and was browsing through rooms when I came to Sir John Everett Millais's *Christ in the House of His Parents*.[111]

I could do better than this. It was like watching an actor pretending to play the cello, that annoying pretence of the fingers and the bow in the wrong place at the wrong time. At least Millais could have got the workshop right. He was too busy with the clunking symbolism. My deaths could be perfect. I could make my darling perfect.

Millais's technique is such that each figure looks as if it's cut out and stuck on the painting. I didn't want that for my darling. Every element would depend on those around it so it wouldn't be possible to say that any piece was individual, though, of course, each piece, like the planks of the yacht I'd seen that day in the port, was made with a singular devotion.

As much as I admire Millais's skills – the fabulous detail, the intricate brushwork which captures, even, the end-grain in the ledges and the scuffs on the workbench – there are elements which, to a craftsman, do not make sense.[112] The nail on which Christ has injured himself

---

[110] It could never be called craftsmanship

[111] It is also known as *The Carpenter's Shop* (1849) but because of the painting's inaccuracies, I cannot think of it in this way

[112] I prefer the craftsmanship in the tabernacle frame: the ornate pediment with its volute and central scallop, the pilaster with urn detail, the architrave's egg and dart carving and the swagged linen in the frieze

has been hammered through one of the planks where it serves no constructional purpose. Yes, it's obvious that the pierced hand which has dripped blood on his foot foretells his crucifixion, and Mary on her knees next to him is how she is in a thousand paintings of the Pietà, but there are more inaccuracies which upset me.

Joseph and the figure opposite him are holding hammers. On the wall behind the six figures, is a frame saw, a 45 x 90 set square, and a leather strap nailed to the wall in which are arranged:

- a small pair of pincers
- a large chisel (the blade is hidden behind Mary's head)
- a firmer chisel
- auger (its tip lost in paint 'mist')[113]
- a hammer (with the profile of a claw hammer)
- a large tool with a handle shaped so as not to roll on the bench
- an unidentified tool (lost behind Christ's head)
- a lump hammer.

There is a pair of pincers on the ledged door on the workbench, too, next to the nail on which Christ has injured himself. It's not clear whether Christ was trying to remove the nail, or if he caught himself on the point protruding underneath. There are another two nails on the door, ready to be hammered through the ledges. Strewn all over the floor are shavings, curling like leaves.[114] And that's another problem: of all the tools in the painting, the one which creates these shavings is absent. There is no plane of any kind in sight.

Ev's clumsiness kept me in Spain far longer than I had expected. I returned to Wales only to reacquaint myself with its other-world and to see Elena. We went to the Halfway which was becoming our place in that way places can become important to lovers. This

---

[113] There is a painting in the Louvre by Georges de La Tour called *St. Joseph the Carpenter* (1645) in which you can see an auger being used. I like the painting because the viewer's eyes focus on the tool itself

[114] These remind me of the leaves in another of Millais's paintings, *Mariana* (1851)

was how I was beginning to think of it. Elena's hand brushed mine and I felt something in my stomach I hadn't felt since before my balls had been smashed.

In the preparatory drawing of the painting the selection of tools is different:

- a large unidentified tool with a shaped handle and blade (hidden behind Mary's head)
- a set square
- auger
- a saw with a curved blade similar to a modern flooring saw
- a tool which looks as if it is heated to bore holes through wood
- a gimlet[115] (partially hidden behind the ladder propped against the wall)
- another unidentified tool (hidden behind Joseph's head).

And in Joseph's hand is a hammer, its claw easily visible. But even in this drawing there is no plane.[116]

There is a problem with the ledged door being constructed on the bench, also. There are three types of battened door: ledged; ledged and braced; framed ledged and braced. Apart from a large single plank placed in an aperture, these are the simplest doors. A ledged door is what Millais is depicting here. The three planks are secured by the ledges – one near the top, one near the bottom and one in the middle – through which nails are hammered and bent over, by striking them with a nail punch at that point where they emerge from

---

[115] A gimlet is similar to a bradawl, used for making holes for nails or screws

[116] There is a lovely wooden smoothing plane in the drawing *Christ in the Carpenter's Workshop* by Carl Müller, made in the same year as that of Millais (it's in the Royal Collection). The shavings it has produced are curling next to it on the end of the bench. Müller's observations of the workshop are actually much better than those of Millais: tusk-tenons have been used to construct the workbench against which a crude G-cramp is propped, and there is even a bench stop against which a plank is butted. Christ is at the centre of the image, ripping down the grain of a plank with a large-toothed saw, slicing across the image diagonally from top left to bottom right

the timber. Millais's door would not last very long, however, because the ledges are too small.

And in the background, timber is stored upright against the wall. Stored like this it will lose its form and be difficult to work.[117] Jesús's wood store (my Jesús that is), was an astonishing array of different species collected over a lifetime of working with wood.

So Millais got the workshop wrong:

- there is a nail in the middle of nowhere
- there are no planes
- the ledges are too small
- the timber storage is impractical.

A ledged door has a tendency to fall out of square. Braces help to maintain square and a frame keeps such constructions rigid. The door members which will be inaccessible are best painted before assembly, that is, all the board contacts, tongues and grooves, ledges and braces. The frame joints are normally glued.

"All of Wales was there," Elena said. "That's what it looked like to me. The chapel was heaving with all the Welsh players and stuff, not that I knew any of them. And they had speakers for the crowds outside. The vicar said some nice things and there were readings by people who'd played with him. There were loads of people I haven't seen for years. It was in all the papers and on the telly."

I nodded at all this.

"The police reckon he was killed by the same person who killed Bull and Dog. Multiple stab wounds. They were more or less in the same place on each of them, apparently. It's like a ritual or something. They haven't seen anything like it before in this country.

"Phew," sounded ridiculous when I replied.

"Who'd've thought," she said, "this place'd be put on the map by a serial killer."

In fact, all of Wales and the world was what I could see from the top of Twmbarlwm, its 360 degrees taking in the peaks of the Brecon

---

[117] It should be racked horizontally. As far as I can tell, the timber is all softwood, too

Beacons to the north and the coast of Devon to the south, the Severn Bridge glinting to the east and Cardiff smoking to the west. It is the most beautiful of all the views I have seen anywhere in the world, where I have closed my eyes and thought of myself as an anemometer spinning in the wind, where I have looked down on *Buteo buteo* gliding over Maes Mawr Farm below and looked up at the *Alauda arvensis*[118] beating against the blue of the sky.

One day I decided to get to the top via the forestry on its southern slope. I climbed over the fence and immediately found myself in a strange place, under the low branches of the firs packed together so tightly that it was dark, so dark and cramped, that I could have been staggering underground as miners did moving from the coalface to the shaft which would haul their bodies back into the light. The needles cushioned my tread but spiked me from the branches so that my hands bled where they had been pricked often. And when I emerged at the nipple of the summit it was as if whatever straps had constricted me were released.

Some would say that all *this* had made me. All of them psychologists. What made me were the three boys whose characters were so deficient that they sought to patch them up with a fourth. And even after they ruined me, continued to attack me with words like stones.

"There are similarities," she said, "the police won't let on about."

"Really?"

"Yeah, they won't say."

There was a lull before she broke the silence again.

"Matt was there too," she said.

"Who's Matt?"

"You know, my first boyfriend. Napper."

"Him."

"Yes. Have a guess what he's doing?" I shrugged.

"Still thinks he's a rock star."

I looked across at her, concentrating on her lips and teeth and tongue, and thought, my God, she's absolutely stunning. I wanted to

[118] Sky lark

put my head in her mouth and pull myself into that moist heat. When her mouth was closed, her lips met like a perfect joint, the outline of the top and bottom lip perfectly aligned. I wondered which species would best present them. I wanted to take out my profile gauge to record them. I made a mental note of how wide her mouth was in relation to her nostrils.

It would be good to kill a rock star.

When I closed my eyes that night I admired the colour and texture of her lips and kissed them without her knowing.

Chapter Eighteen

Giovani di Paolo's *Saints Fabian and Sebastian*[119] is crude. Art historians probably describe it as naïve. Perhaps. It captures the Saint Sebastian story with some horror, though, his torso being pierced by twenty arrows. Some would say that they are randomly placed as such an execution might occur. For me, this is what I dislike: I want them to be more precise. As arrows, they are ridiculously short, too.

"You don't abuse the hammer and you don't abuse the nail," Jesús said. "They have a relationship which must be respected."

He held a piece of sandpaper on a flat surface with his left hand, held the 24 oz claw hammer by its handle with his right and, keeping the head's face against the paper, pushed it back and for whilst pressing it down.

"There," he said, showing me the shining face. "Then you need to clean the adjoining edge, like this."

He wrapped the paper around the head with his left hand and turned the hammer around like a crank with his right.

"This is what I want you to do." He cramped a length of scrap timber[120] to the bench, selected about a hundred nails of different types and sizes. "I want you to hit these in."

He left me alone.

Easy.

When he came back he nodded and smiled at what I'd done. I'd tried to hammer them in a straight line along the timber.

"You have bent them and there are more pennies[121] than a kid's piggy bank."

He made me do it again the next day and the next day and the next day until I hit in each nail cleanly. "Hold the handle at the end

---

[119] About 1475. The National Gallery

[120] At this point I didn't know the names of the timbers

[121] This describes the mark the hammer head leaves on the wood, like a pre-decimal penny. It is essential not to mark the timber

of the shaft and use your wrist as the fulcrum. Don't grip the handle too tightly."

For the next piece he said, "You must be able to control a specific hammer for a specific purpose."

He took a pin hammer and a handful of one-inch panel pins, which he hit into the timber without stopping, the next pin between his finger and thumb in readiness. As soon as the pin head was flush with the timber surface he started the next. He didn't make one error, his swing perfect. "It's the weight of the head which needs to do the work. Eye on the nail, not the hammer. Keep a rhythm and never rush. Now you."

He set me similar exercises with saws: "Lift the blade slightly on the back stroke or it'll catch. Blow the dust away from the line as you cut." As the blade wandered from the line he said, "Imagine your arm is on a steam engine." I practised with a tenon saw, a dovetail saw, a gentleman's saw, the teeth getting finer, the kerf smaller, the accuracy greater.

Crivelli's *La Madonna della Rondine*[122] is most interesting, though. In the predella[123] are three separate paintings: St. Jerome in the wilderness, the Nativity and the Martyrdom of St. Sebastian. Sebastian is strung up with rope to a tree. He is lifted onto one foot and appears to be in a machine. The rope binds his left arm around his back. There are three arrows: one in his left elbow, one in the swell of his abdomen just below the navel and one through his right foot. Facing him are the three executioners. The nearest to him is holding a bow, left-handed so that the viewer can see the bow itself, then there is a right-handed man with a crossbow and the last man's bow is straight.

I couldn't take seriously the first Spanish police officer I saw because he had long hair protruding from under his cap and a paunch which he seemed to heave out of his car. I didn't like his brown two-tone uniform, either, which made him look like an advertisement for bad fashion. Yet he had a pistol.

---

[122] "Madonna of the Swallow" about 1490–2. The National Gallery
[123] The painted tier below an altarpiece

The city police wore blue and appeared friendlier. The Guardia Civil looked like soldiers in their high boots, berets and dark glasses. They carried machine guns.

"The hammer and saw are the basics. If you can handle them you're on your way," Jesús said, holding a Stanley No. 5 jack plane. "You've got to make one of these sing."

He butted a 6' length of timber against the bench stop. Then he lifted the plane and turned it over so that he was sighting along its sole,[124] and took a shaving the whole length of the timber to a *sheesh.* "That's singing." He unfurled the shaving, fine and delicate as a veil, along the timber to show that it matched exactly. He picked up a No. 4½ smoothing plane. "Watch."

He altered his stance and pushed hard into the stroke. The plane juddered. Jesús pulled me close to look at the result. The grain was ripped up, the shaving broken. "That's what you get if the iron's blunt and not set up correctly." He turned over the plane to show me the chipped iron.

I had also met the security at the airport. My hand baggage set off the alarm when it went through X-ray. The guard pointed his machine gun at me and hailed me to one side without speaking. He stood to one side watching me empty the bag for another officer. My grandfather's plane had singled me out.

Jesús showed me how to sharpen chisels.

My body and mind had to come together in a conjoined memory, the angle and size of each chisel in my hands pressing into a part of my mind as if into wet grey cement.

Jesús made me cut housings with a variety of bevel-edged chisels, from 1½" to 3/8". Each had to be the width of the chisel I was using. I marked the housing across the surface of the timber and used a tenon saw to cut to the floor of the housing, half-way through the timber. Then I had to chop out. "All by hand," he said. He showed me.

---

[124] He was adjusting the iron with the depth-adjustment nut and the lateral adjustment lever, I would learn

"When the chisel's sharp enough you will be able to push it through the grain. If it's tough, strike the handle with the ball of your hand. Don't go straight through the housing, or there's a risk of splitting the grain. Go half-way, turn the piece around and repeat." He took a combination square to check that the housing was the same depth for its entire width. "It's okay to have a *slight* hollow but not a rise, because then you'll have gaps."

I began to appreciate the beauty of the tools, their weight and purpose. My great works needed great skills. My great skills needed great tools.

Chapter Nineteen

"This is it," the surgeon said, putting the implant into my hand. "It's silicon gel in a silicon shell. Three sizes. This one should do you."

"Is this what I had before?"

"More or less. They're very good as far as size and weight are concerned."

"What about erections? I haven't had any erections."

"Well, studies show that patients feel better about themselves when they have the implants than if they do not."

"That didn't answer the question."

"Well, no. They won't help your erectile function directly."

"What will?"

"As far as I can see, there is nothing physically preventing you from having an erection."

"It's psychological."

"That's how it presents itself."

"And when might this change?"

"I think you have to realise that the further you get away from the trauma without experiencing an erection the less likely it is you will have one again."

I squeezed the implant in my hand so that it looked as if it might pop. "Tough, aren't they?" I put it back into his hands, the hands that had repaired me, trimmed the damage, tied tubes, sewn me neatly. And here they were in the air between us, explaining procedure, with the band of gold on one finger, his electricity.

"They really are very good."

"I thought they'd be glass."[125]

"Oh, yes, glass has been used, as has Lucite, Dacron and Gellfoam. These are the most commonly available now."

"No tubes."

---

[125] In the film *Ensign Pulver* the eponymous hero (Robert Walker Jr.) implants sterile glass into the Captain (Burl Ives)

"They are purely cosmetic. They'll fill your scrotum rather than having that bag of skin behind your penis."

"I think I'd prefer to be left as I am. It's not actually going to give me what I want."

"You experienced a dreadful trauma," he said. "I understand."

I wondered how many times a doctor might say *I understand* during their career when the words were as empty as my scrotal sac.

"You don't have to make the decision now. Go away and think about it and if you decide that, in fact, you would like to go ahead with the implants, then let us know."

The empty shell and the tortoise head that never emerged would be the constant reminder of my reason for being and doing.

Dovetail Joints: Marking Tails

For a through dovetail joint, accurately cut each component to be joined. Plane the ends square using a shooting board. Mark the shoulder for the tails with a try square and pencil. Then mark the tails. Generally, the tails should be of equal size and spacing. Mark the tails on the face side with a dovetail template or sliding bevel. It is a good idea to mark the waste to avoid errors.

I had been standing outside Elena's door for a while after knocking when Napper opened it. I hoped my face didn't register the surprise.

"Tim!" he said.

I stepped back and looked up. "I'm sorry, I think I must have the wrong house."

"Hi Sebastian," Elena said, appearing behind Napper. "I was in the loo."

"Oh, hi. Thought I had the wrong place for a moment."

We stood on the threshold.

"It *is* Tim," Elena said to Napper.

"Oh, right," said Napper. He held out his hand. "It's good to see you again."

I held out my hand. "Again?" I said, affecting an innocent voice and puzzled face.

"Yes, yes, Napper. Matthew Rand."

I feigned a penny dropping. "Ah, Elena's boyfriend. I remember."

Cutting Tails

Position the tail component in the vice so that one side of each tail is vertical. This will make cutting with the dovetail saw easier. Be careful not to go beyond the shoulder line. Re-position the component, repeat on the other side of the tails.

Now set the component in the vice horizontally. Cut out the corner waste. A coping saw will remove most of the waste from between the tails. Then place the component flat and pare out with a chisel. Remember to work from both sides to the middle to prevent break out, and finish to the shoulder line.

"I thought you might have remembered me for other reasons."

"Oh, yes. Well. That was a long time ago. Kids and stuff."

"So, how are you now? I mean, you know," Napper said.

"Yes, fine."

"I never said sorry."

"No."

He gave a small nervous laugh. "That was me trying to say sorry, I think. I know it's not much?"

"No, not much."

"I'm sorry," he said again.

We were still on the threshold.

"Yes, you said." Sorry on a doorstep, Elena's doorstep, the girl for whom my boyhood craving was now un-electrified love. "Well, good to see you. I'll be getting on." He walked down the path to his car.

"Bye!" Elena called after him. "God, I'd have done anything for him when I was a kid," she said to herself.

I saw her as a fifteen-year-old undressing for him, her blue bra and pants. I wanted to kill him immediately.

Marking Pins

To mark the pins some craftsmen actually paint the end grain of the prepared component with weak white paint, or rub

chalk into it. Put it in the vice vertically. Position the cut tail member on top, ensuring the face marks correspond. Line up the edges and tails' shoulder lines precisely on the painted/chalked end and mark them with a knife. Square down the lines to the shoulders on each face and mark the waste.

The newspaper stories could be a problem. If they revealed too much then Napper might become more aware of unusual situations in which he *might* find himself. It could complicate things, too. And if he knew the manner in which Bull, Dog and Ev had died, my darling might cause him to react in a way which would risk the correct and satisfying outcome when they met.

It was difficult for me to remember that it wasn't going to be as easy as making my darling and seeing her love them. Jesús's exercises weren't just about getting things right, they were also about patience. Every little thing – each hammer blow, each saw stroke – was something to contemplate. I had my project. I had my skills. I had all the time necessary to make my goal achievable. There was no rush. It would happen. But I had to keep in mind that the lives of those who were going to make my life's work complete were variable. Not only had I to consider my darling, I had to evaluate their particular contribution.

It would have been ludicrous to rush in and see what happened. It wasn't about being caught; it was about achieving my goal. I only lived for my great work, for justice.

Cutting the Pins
Set each component in the vice vertically. Saw down to the shoulder line, following the lines marked from the tails. The saw must be kept to the waste side, just touching the marked line. Use a coping saw to remove most of the waste between the pins. Cut to the shoulder line with a chisel, again from both sides to the middle. Clean corners with the chisel at the same angle as the pins.

"Coffee?"

"Not unless it's the real stuff," I said, not meaning to sound rude.

"Oh. No. It's Nescafé. It's good though," Elena said. Her response hurt just as much as if I had intended to be rude. Nescafé: I mean, where would I start?

"I'll have tea."

She brought the cups through and sat opposite me. "Fancy Matt popping in when you called."

"Yeah."

"It's always good to see him." She looked towards the window and was smiling.

If only she knew. I could tell her now. Everything. The coldness that gripped me when they ripped down my trousers; the dig of the biro in my back; that strange nausea before passing out. Waking to find I had no balls and knowing that she had seen me like that.

"Mmm."

"I'm sorry. I keep forgetting you didn't like that lot, did you?"

"Not really."

She changed tack. "How's your work?"

"Good. Busy."

"I meant your special project thing."

"Surprised you remember that. Yes, that too. I'm pleased with it."

"You've been working on that a while."

"It's an ongoing thing, you know."

"So what do you do with it exactly?"

"It's hard to explain. It's a work of art, I suppose. That's the best way to describe it."

"Like a sculpture kind of thing?"

I was pleased she'd come up with that. It made me feel as if we *could* share something. "I suppose so."

"I'd like to see it. Afraid I haven't got the money to come out to Spain, though."

"One day, perhaps."

She smiled a half-believing smile.

Assembly

Dovetails are meant to be extremely tight fitting and assembled as few times as possible. You should try to do it once only.

Partly assemble the joint and trim tight spots. Clean all inside faces before gluing. You should apply glue to both components, then tap the joint together. Use a piece of waste timber to protect the surface.

If it is a wide dovetail joint, make sure that you tap evenly across the component in order to keep it level. Wipe away surplus glue. When dry, clean up the joint with a smoothing plane, from the edges to the middle to prevent break out.

Chapter Twenty

We were sitting in Café del Mar after church with the doors open to the blue sky and harbour.

"So," Jesús said, leaving that opener hang for a considerable time before continuing. "What are you doing?"

He had not asked before but had merely looked and nodded. What I did in my time didn't concern him as long as it did not interfere with the commissions. The workshop's size was such that my darling did not compromise the work space and I paid for all the timber I used or ordered.

"Doing?"

"Your work. What is it?" That neuter pronoun reduced my darling to two small letters.[126] Jesús had a way of finding the essence of a design and transposing it into a project but now he had minimalised – even at the stage my darling had reached then – my investment. *It*. An object. My darling wasn't *it*. She was dynamic and beautiful. She had grace and poise. She had meaning. "It's vulgar," Jesús said. He was looking into the blue.

"I think it's beautiful," I said, weakly defending myself and unfortunately using *it* again.

"Oh, yes, the craftsmanship is good." He continued looking into the blue. Then he turned to me. "But the concept is vulgar." He took a sip of coffee.

It. Vulgar. That adjective immediately created *Sturnus vulgaris*, dirtily domestic, the plebeian on the make, the bird with no voice of its own.[127]

"I did not teach you vulgarity," he said.

I felt nauseous. The man to whom I had given myself had reduced my dear-Est to something ordinary.

"She is not vulgar," I said.

---

[126] And an insignificant voice print, the ineffectual [l] followed by the voiceless alveolar plosive [t]

[127] Starlings are well known for their ability to imitate other birds and sounds

"*She*! It's a woman now! Since when have I ever called anything other than what it is?" He was shouting. Gregorio looked over from the counter.

I didn't know what to say.

"*She*," he said again, shaking his head. "We work on projects that will have long lives, we hope, but they aren't *alive*."

I didn't know what to look at. Gregorio lifted his head slightly and flashed his eyebrows as if to ask what was going on. I didn't respond.

"And what is *she* going to do? *She* is for something, isn't *she*?" The pronouns pierced me like arrows.

Now *I* looked out into the blue. There was nothing out there. He stood up and sipped the last of his coffee, looked at me and walked out.

I stayed in the café for most of the day looking into the blue for an answer. The rich of Gijón were playing on their yachts and boats. A fisherman unloaded his catch at the restaurant at the port wall. I nodded another coffee from Gregorio.

"What's happening with Jesús?" he said.

"I don't know."

The coffee was bitter.

"Who is it for?" Jesús asked.

It again. "For me."

"You are not making it for yourself."

"Me," I insisted.

"*You* are going to use it?"

"One day."

"But it's not *for* you."

"It is."

"Will *you* sit on it?"

"No."

"Then *who* will?"

"I can't tell you."

"Won't tell me."

I didn't respond.

"I did not teach you to do such things."

"I am not doing it with you in mind at all. It's all from me."

"You *have* made something beautiful," he said, "but I don't like it."

"It is designed to be beautiful at the moment someone sits on it."

"No no no. Our pieces are of themselves. They must not need anything else." Jesús shook his head. "Our work must speak for itself. It does not need a dialogue of any kind. You cannot do this."

I had left him behind. His attitude was old-fashioned and I realised his philosophy of stand-alone craftsmanship was wrong. We stood in silence for a while before I eventually picked up a brush and started sweeping the floor.

It was wrong not to consider how our pieces could live other than transposing them from a drawing to three dimensions only. To understand that each element merely went to make a large component which, when interacting and assessing the addition of another, would only be complete at that instant, was beyond Jesús. It was a shame. It was like Webb's *Red House*. Each door, each window, each tread of the stairs was merely an element of the component, and the component meant nothing without people to give it meaning. This is what I was making. And in the moment at which it lived it would take life. It was the *instant* of craftsmanship. The edge on which my whole self balanced.

I wanted to hear the fall but it was like being on top of Twmbarlwm the way the breeze whipped off the sea past my ears. I made sure Jesús's ID card was in his pocket when I took him to the cliff and rolled him over the edge onto the rocks and stones below. It was ignoble yet a necessity I had been forced into. *Vulgar. It.* There was no need to take anything from him because he had given me everything I needed and could not give more. "'*Porque de tal manera amó Dios al mundo, que la dado á su Hijo unigénito, para que todo aquel que en él cree, no se pierda, mas tenga vida eternal,*'" I said.

I struck him with the *lignum vitae* mallet he used for carving. I saw his face in the mirror of his latest project (for a Spanish client) as I came up behind him. He smiled at me. I smiled back, and swung the mallet just as he'd taught me. There was a 'thwok' as it connected with the back of his head and he crumpled to the floor. It was satisfyingly clean. The injury to his head would be lost in the multiple injuries of the cliff fall. The police merely came to tell me he had been found and asked me to identify him. I guessed *Larus argentatus*[128] had taken his eyes. It was his hands, actually, which told me it was him.

It hurt to make his coffin. It felt as though I had Jesús in my hands, struck as I was by the weight of each tool in my hands: Stanley No. 4 smoother, his liver; 1¼" chisel, his heart; Stanley No 3. smoother, his brain; all contained in the Stanley No. 5½ jack plane of his skin, flayed. Every now and then I could hear Jesús's voice saying *vulgar*, but I was confident that he would agree that the decorative through dovetails were magnificent on such wide boards. The undertaker said it was handsome.

There were candles burning in small red glasses in the darkness of the chapel when I arrived but there was no one about. I waited. Then I stood in the doorway looking out onto the landscape. The fields were as green as any I had ever seen. There were heavy charcoal clouds on the mountains but with the sun behind them they did not look threatening. Two small tractors phutted in the distance.

The undertakers arrived. The coffin was wonderful. The sky was huge. The priest and the undertaker shook my hand and left. I sat in the chapel and cried until the candles burned out. I walked home.

The only good to come of Jesús's death was that his tools became mine. Every day I had seen them in his hands. I had used them when I had first arrived until I could build up a set of my own but that had been years before. Holding them now I could not help but feel Jesús guiding my hands, ensuring that what I did was true.

The undertakers had kindly allowed me a week to make the coffin,

---

[128] Herring Gull

being quite fascinated by the trouble to which I put myself. I took them in to the workshop to see Jesús's work.

"He will not be comfortable[129] in our coffin," the undertaker proclaimed seriously.

I spent two days preparing his tools. It took so long because each craftsman sharpens their irons at an angle specific to them if they do not use a honing guide. The irons had to 'fit' me, so I had to re-grind the base angle for some of the planes. I sharpened and cleaned them and lay them out on his bench. Seeing the planes arranged side by side[130] was quite something. They were imbued with years of handling, had shaped and finished the most incredible pieces rather than being factory-crisp and unfettled. Their irons had been sharpened to take the hairs from the back of a hand, their soles trued the grain of a multitude of timbers.

I felt calm after Jesús died. I could work unhindered. I continued to work on commissions as my darling developed. The moment at which she would astonish me was not to be rushed and her winged presence in the workshop, was, at times, comforting. Jesús had brought me as far as he could and now I was exploring craftsmanship's greater possibilities.

Sometimes I would sit and hold one of his tools – the Norris No. 5, for instance – and remember how he took it apart, sharpened the iron, put it back together, sighted down the sole and made it sing on a piece of timber.

---

[129] *Cómodo* in Spanish. I liked the sound of this, too, especially how it moved to the bed of the unstressed syllables

[130] Norris No. 5 with rosewood infill, Norris 20 7/8" steel adjustable jointer with rosewood infill and handle, Stanley No. 5½ jack plane, Stanley No. 3 smoother, Stanley No. 4 smoother, Norris 10 5/8" No. 11 mitre plane with rosewood infill, Norris No. 50G adjustable steel soled gunmetal coffin smoother with walnut infill, Stanley No. 55 combination plane, Stanley No 20. compass plane, Stanley No 80. scraper plane, Stanley No. 71 router plane, Stanley No. 601/2 low angle block plane, Stanley No. 98 & No. 99 left and right side rebate planes, Record 077A bull-nose plane, Preston gunmetal shoulder rabbet plane

There was no greeting on the card from Salamanca:

I want you to come to New York. I've told Mom and Dad all about you and they're excited to meet you. There's so much to see! I'll take you to all the places I know you'll love, show you wonderful things: Frank Lloyd Wright's[31] drawings, Wyeth[32], Hopper[33] (like Spain without the warmth) and the Chrysler. Then when we've had enough we can just sit in a bar. Won't be like Café Jazz but I promise it'll be good. Coffee-cup of love, Stacey xxxxxxx

Then she arrived, having contacted me after Jesús died. She also wanted what I didn't have to give. I should have realised why she was coming to see me.

I had never been greeted by a naked woman on entering a room. That she was so attractive added to the misery. I stopped and looked. She smiled. "Well?" My mind immediately went to my penis, as if to say, What do *you* think? No answer. Deaf and dumb, maybe. "Well?" she said again.

"Beautiful," I replied.

She stretched her arms above her head and lifted herself up on tip-toes in a well-practised exercise, then turned. "I used to do this in ballet." I took in her design, the muscles in her back, the defined calf, the xylophone of her ribs. She stopped and held out her hands to me. "Please."

I stepped forward. She stretched up and kissed me. I tried.

"What is it?"

"I can't do this," I said. I felt as if there was no option but to walk out.

"Sebastian," she said, "please."

---

[31] Architect (1867-1959), whose designs are crisp and precise

[32] Andrew Wyeth, (1917 –), artist. I particularly enjoy the buildings in his paintings. I have imagined myself in "Weatherside" (1965) many times

[33] Edward Hopper (1882 – 1967), artist. Stacey was very fond of his painting *Nighthawks* (1942). I preferred his etchings, especially *Night Shadows* (1921)

"I told you. I can't do this," I found myself saying again a day later when she came into *my* room. She pulled me gently to the bed and began undoing my belt. She stood back from me and undressed. She undid the buttons of her yellow linen shirt and let it hang open as she stepped out of her skirt. Then she pushed her shoulders back and let the shirt slip down her arms. She stood in front of me, glowing in the light coming through the window. "I can't," I said.

"Let me." She knelt in front of me and unbuckled my belt.

I closed my eyes tight. She put me on my back and pulled at my pants. She stopped and there was silence.

"What happened?"

"I was only a boy," I said.

"What happened?"

"I was beaten up."

"Oh my God." She touched me.

I looked down at my penis, helpless as a *Parus caeruleus* hatchling in her hands.

"Why didn't you tell me?"

"I couldn't."

"It's not fair. You *should* have told me."

"Yes."

She kissed my penis as if she could bring it to life. "Poor love."

We lay on the bed looking at the ceiling and I listened to her breathing. Then I looked at her. I liked the shape of her breasts when she lay back. "Can I touch you?"

She smiled.

I curved my hand so that it matched the curve of her breast where it hung over her ribs. I ran the tips of my fingers slowly over her abdomen.

"I'm sorry I can't give you what you want."

"Did you lie to me?" she said.

"I haven't lied to you."

"You said you were in love with someone else. Was that because you didn't want to tell me about what happened?"

"No. Yes. Both."

She sighed and looked at the ceiling. She cried silently. Then she looked at me. "There is something you can give me."

"I can't."

"Make me something."

"What?"

"You decide. Something of you."

We put our arms around each other.

"I'll make you something," I said, and we went to sleep.

I woke in the morning to find the place next to me empty, Stacey's form printed on the sheet. I could smell coffee. It was new to me, this domesticity, the simplicity of living with a person whom one might love. It was how I had imagined things could be with Elena one day. You shared a bed with someone, breakfasted together, went to work, then joined each other again. The notion of living like this, attached by the elastic of love which stretched then pulled you back, was exciting.

In the kitchen the table was set with egg cups, croissants were warming in the oven and the coffee pot was steaming. I turned off the gas. Stacey would be in with the eggs shortly.

She didn't come so I went to find her. She had left the egg basket at the door to the workshop, which was open. I don't understand why, but I half-expected to find her at the bench, creating a version of her self. She wasn't. The door to my great work was open and there was Stacey, an egg in each hand broken in the snatch of death.

She had given me so much and I had given her nothing. My life's work had burgled her essence, so that all that balanced in front of me was the empty representation of a grand design, a great house without its contents.

It wasn't clear whether it was an accident or not. Yes, she was dead. Yes, she was killed by that to which I had devoted myself. She *couldn't* have known that this wonderful design would weigh her then steal from her. My sweet-Est's timbers *sensed* the time to act.

There was no point checking that she might be alive. My angel had done what she was designed to do perfectly. It intrigued me that

I had missed this moment of beauty. Though ultimately unsatisfactory, it must have been something extraordinary.

The Conductor appeared. He ran a small piece of cedar under his nose like a fine cigar. **You see, monsieur, you have done another terrible thing.**

"It wasn't me."

Your machine, monsieur. She may as well have died by your own hand.

"The 'machine'- as you call it – reacted as it was designed to."

She was innocent.

"It wasn't planned."

You must stop what you are doing.

"She didn't suffer."

Monsieur, you are a monster. You should sit on your own chair.

Oh how it angered me to hear this fop say 'chair'. "Would you like to join me?"

He scowled. **It is not right that you should use your talent in such a terrible way. You have a gift which you can use for joy and wonder, yet you insist on this preposterous and cruel venture.**

He was a persistent boor. No wonder the revolutionaries had separated his head and body. "You say that I have talent then insult me by saying that my work is preposterous and cruel."

That is correct.

"It is neither. It is as efficient as the guillotine and there is no suffering."

What about the suffering of those left behind?

"That has nothing at all to do with my work. My angel is for a moment with an individual. That is why I conceived her. Nothing else."

Your angel, as you say, is not doing any good at all.

"The opinion of a Frenchman from the period of the revolution, when furniture announced itself with opulent swags of gilt, cannot be taken seriously."

You patronise, monsieur. You have no manners. I fear you shall go to the other place, surely. He pronounced this like a threat.

"I am Sebastian. I am a great craftsman. I make masterpieces of trees."

The Conductor vanished.

Chapter Twenty-one

I opened the window.

"We don't see many of these on the road around here," the officer said, referring first to the van and then the number plate.

"Don't suppose you do," I said. "What's the problem?"

"No problem, sir, just fancied a look, that's all," he said. "You don't sound Spanish."

"From around here, actually. I live in Spain now though."

"Can't keep away, eh?" he laughed.

"Something like that."

"I know where I'd rather be."

"That's what most people say. I live in the north. It's similar to here."

"You've gone and spoiled my picture of you in the sun."

"So what's this then?" he said, tapping the side of the van.

"It's an HY."[134]

"Yes, I know. 1947 to 1981. I've got a Dinky one of these I had when I was a kid but this is the first I've seen. Mind if I take a look?" He nodded to the back.

I got out of the driver's seat and unlocked the back doors for him. I had to pretend indifference as I did so, concealing the thrill I felt each time I saw what was revealed. There she was, in pieces, wrapped in blankets and stored carefully in the space.

"What's all this?"

"I make furniture."

"Ah. Can I see?"

I unwrapped a component for him.

"Wow. Proper furniture. Don't know anyone who'd want this round here."

"You'd be surprised."

"Sure I would, sure I would."

I wrapped it again and closed the doors.

---

[134] Citroën

He looked over the van, glanced at the documents in the windscreen, tapped a tyre with his foot. "Nice. Mind how you go."

As he pulled away I thought of his boyhood toys ranged on shelves in a spare room. I drove on with the angel in my van.

Now when I returned to Wales it was for two reasons: to see Elena and kill Napper. My visits became more and more measured. I had to get it right. I could barely contemplate what it would mean if things went wrong and I could barely comprehend what ecstasy awaited me when I got it right. It would be the instant to which I had been working since the warm afternoon my lovely fifteen-year-old self became 1½oz lighter. I had been robbed by a gang of which Napper was the ring leader, the prize. The moment at which my darling loved him would be the zenith of craftsmanship. The privilege would be extraordinary. The bounds of craftsmanship would be pushed further and I would be the only person there to witness it, the person responsible for its conception and execution, though that noun hardly seemed a fair appraisal of the enormous event.

But measured it had to be. The other deaths had been unsatisfactory and I was cognisant that I could jeopardise my final opportunity to get things right by my eagerness and frustration. Jesús's philosophy of re-making rather than making-do had taught me to get things right, and there was no room for errors, no second chance.

So I kept away from Napper. I had to wait.

I walked the canal and visited the spot where I had been emasculated. I hugged my *Quercus robur* and wept into its bark. I could feel it drawing nourishment from deep in the earth and radiating its might into my arms. A *Turdus ericetorum* called in the branches above my head as if it were the whistle of this huge and gentle machine.

I looked up through the crown of branches through which the sun fell, spilling from leaf to leaf to the ground. The tree which had unwittingly been the post to which I had been tied would become a part of my darling's expression. I changed my mind about it being inappropriate. It was essential for it to be a part of my darling.

I returned early the next morning with the tools necessary to take what I wanted back to Spain, where I had to convert and season it.

That took time.[135] I could have rushed it in a kiln but air seasoning is far superior.

I was standing in front of Rubens's *St. Sebastian*[136] in the Staatliche Museum, Berlin when the French accent broke the silence in which I was enveloped.

That was not his time, it said.

I turned to see the Conductor. "What are you doing here?"

Ah, mon amie, it is you who I should be asking that question. He was dressed in the uniform of the museum's guards but had a clipboard and cane. **It's getting close to your time,** he said, tapping the board.

"It isn't. I've got my work to do. I must finish my work."

You are a wicked man. If you come with me now, you will not fall into the arms of my cousin. And believe me, monsieur, you do not want to meet him. He is from deep in the south, an altogether uncouth man, he shivered. He took the handkerchief from his breast pocket and pressed it under each eye, then flicked it at me. **You wicked man,** and he turned, his heels clacking on the floor as he walked away.

The Conductor appeared at the Monasterio de Santa María de Valdediós[137] to which I had travelled for the day to see Andrés Gonzáles's *St. Sebastian*. Sebastian's proportions are poor, the torso too large, the head cranked and looking as if it should be on another body altogether.

Mon amie, Sebastian again?

I was not surprised this time. I didn't even turn to acknowledge him. I felt like a nonchalant Cary Grant[138] who could dismiss him with a supercilious remark if I so wished.

---

[135] It takes approximately one year for each one inch thickness if drying hardwood and half that for softwood

[136] 200 x 120 cm (1614). What is most interesting about the painting is the horn knock on the bow curling next to Sebastian's right knee. It is similar to a cello scroll in shape

[137] Villaviciosa, Asturias, Spain

[138] He is particularly good in Alfred Hitchcock's *North by Northwest* (1959), a 3000–mile chase

What is this Sebastian thing?

"I identify with him."

He was a saint. On the other hand you are none such.

"I am a craftsman."

No monsieur, you are a murderer. You must stop and repent and then you may come with me.

"I am a craftsman who must complete his work."

We were talking at odds and our roles had reversed. It was I who was in the colourful world talking in black and white terms; he was from that place beyond the instant to which I had dedicated myself, yet he was colourful in argument. There was nothing he could do for me.

Because my testicles had been removed it was as if the fuse which gave me the power to love had been taken out. And something in my brain that could repair the circuit over time could not make the connection. I knew I did love Elena because I wanted to be with her all of the time and when I knew I was going to see her my stomach churned and my skin prickled. My organs had reacted similarly to Stacey but I made a deliberate decision not to permit the feelings to dictate to me: if I had done so, then it could have interfered with what I had set out to do.

At the Museo Lázaro Galdeano[139] he tapped me on the shoulder causing me to turn. The look on my face must have said it all.

Ah, you are not pleased to see me.

"No."

But you must be. I am offering to help you and you keep turning me away.

"You cannot help me."

But monsieur, you are my project.

"My project is more important."

Killing innocent people is wicked.

"They are not innocent!" I shouted.

---

[139] Madrid

A group of women shuffled away quickly. A museum guard approached me. "You must be quiet," he said.

I apologised. The Conductor stood beside him, flicked his handkerchief and bowed extravagantly. I turned to look at Juan de la Abadia's *St. Sebastian*, a sumptuous and vibrant painting of a man in rich clothes and crowned with a layered golden nimbus, a bow in his left hand and arrow held delicately in the right. He could have been considering revenge himself.

And because the Conductor had appeared when I had gone to visit a specific Sebastian, I *expected* to see him, but that would have been too easy for the wily Frenchman. That he did not appear when I went on one of my trips disappointed me. When he did appear it annoyed me. I lived with this floating anxiety.

He did appear, though, when I was standing before the Jesse Tree[140] in Abergavenny. I wanted to take in the rest of the treasures first, so that I could give myself over completely when I saw it.

I thought I heard footsteps behind me but there was no one to be seen. And when I sat in the choir stalls and admired the initials carved naively in the thick warm board in front of me – W.D. 1751, I.H. 1764, H.W. 1768 and the bolder P.A. Phillips 1810 and John Hornblower 176–, disturbed perhaps before he could complete the year – a distinct waft of perfume troubled me. Although I could appreciate the alabaster carvings in the Herbert Chapel, I was most interested in the wood carvings. The creatures guarding the choir stalls were fantastic and entirely in keeping with the medieval world: lions and dragons. One of the latter had a neck and body carved as a spiral, ending in a tail pointed like an arrow, and there was a lion with a mane as impenetrable as chain-mail.

When I reached the Jesse I was stunned to find it had been carved from a single trunk! My first reaction was to stand it up and hug it just as I had hugged the tree on the canal. After all the years it had been

[140] At St. Mary's Parish Church. It is a fifteenth-century depiction of King David's father. It would have formed the base of an enormous carving, a reredos depicting Jesse's descendants like a family tree. The Virgin and Child would have been prominent, and Christ in Glory would have surmounted it. All of this would have been brilliantly painted

on its plinth being admired (or not) by generations, it could give me strength. The man who carved it – I am sure it was one man – had worked with the best tools of the time, chipping away at this huge log to create a patriarch with crisp hooded eyes, a full lip and curling beard.

Ah, King David's father.

I ignored the voice.

What about Sebastian?

"I wanted to see this carving."

Monsieur, it is just an old tree.

I turned to face him. "C'est un idiot," I said.

He looked at me outraged and pouted his garish lips. **Monsieur!**

"Go away."

It is you who must go.

An old woman with an intensely white face and lipstick similar to the Conductor appeared from behind a curtained area with flowers in her hands. "Anything the matter?"

"No, everything's fine."

"Only I thought I heard voices."

I looked around as if to say, *You're hearing things.*

"Oh." She bowed slightly and walked away.

"She can't have long to go," I whispered to myself.

She will live to one hundred and three and die in a nursing home.

I ignored him. I went behind the Jesse. It was hollowed out, and there was a large hand-made nail which had been flattened where it emerged, as well as worm holes and decay which had been dealt with a long time ago. Emerging from the middle of his body was a trunk he supported with his left hand, taking the weight of the ancestors who would have been spread out above him.

You can come with me now and meet all of Jesse's family.

"When I have finished my job."

If you finish, mon amie, you will *not be able to come with me*.

"Then leave me alone, because I must finish what I set out to do."

The old woman was standing behind me when I turned around. "Are you sure you're all right?"

"Fine thanks."

"Have you a particular interest?"

"I like the carvings," I said.

"Oh, yes, we've got nice carvings."

I wondered how old she was now and when she would be going into the nursing home.

I am warning you.

I glared at him.

I had the van in the car park and wanted to take the Jesse with me, not for the piece itself but for the craftsmanship it oozed. I could have put it in the workshop back home and it could have lent itself to my purpose. Its size precluded the possibility. The effigy of Sir John de Hasting whom, the label said, died in 1342, was possible. He was life-size and not fixed to the tomb. I could have just walked straight out with him. The folds of his tunic conveyed the weight of the material masterfully. The legs crossed over each other and rested on a lion which had lost its head over the years but its paws indicated a more accurate representation than the one on the choir stalls. It was likely that Hasting's craftsman had seen a lion rather than guessed at what it looked like from a second or third-hand description.

Chapter Twenty-two

It had annoyed clients that we had no telephone. "We don't need one," Jesús said. "It's a distraction. People would be phoning us all the time and interrupting the work about which they were calling."

It ensured that all our work was done through mail. Jesús would go through the mail himself when I first arrived and I would learn about the commissions through him. Then as I became more useful and gained more proficiency in all aspects of the work, he began to show me the occasional correspondence. I envied him this little ritual every day, when he would open each request not knowing what project might be inside, and which ones appealed enough for him to take on. Then it would be sketched and drawn and made. It could be many months from the arrival of such a letter to the project's completion.

I asked him how he chose a commission.

"It's something immediate," he said. "I get an image of the piece as a whole first, then how individual features might look, which excite me."

"How you will make them?"

"Yes. I can see the colours and textures and shapes of the species I can use. It's like having a dictionary of techniques from which I then start sketching." He unpeeled a sketch he had taped to the drawing board. "See, this is what struck me about this project." He showed me a flight of drawers, the *Dalburgia cearensis* drawer front inlaid with *Acer pseudoplatanus* and dovetails that were half through and half stopped. "I start with things like this and it grows from there. Each decision I make has consequences for what follows. If I change one element, what follows changes."

My dedication was also my salvation, the moment when Napper died, my redemption. The task I had set myself as a boy and pursued with monastic diligence since, would allow me to live again, to begin a new life with Elena. When she said she would do anything for him that day, her face was just the same as when we were teenagers. A long time ago.

I would be a father to her children and pass on my skills. I would make wonderful things without my darling worrying my every thought. Slotted and jointed to everything I did, what would those voids be replaced by? I would be an even better craftsman, endowed with a greater capacity for new works. I would make things beyond the majesty of my darling. I would be a great maker. My work would be incredible.

Jesús's account of how a piece first came to him was something I experienced only when I knew how tools behaved in my hands and had enough skills with which to carry out my ideas. What you see in woodworking books is only sufficient for the enthusiast and gives no insight into what the *craft* is.

Take cutting a dovetail, for instance. In the books the joints are perfect. In reality it takes a great deal of practice to achieve such perfection. There is no mention of what it *feels* like to mark out the joint, or *know* the weight and balance of the tools before you even try to do what you are meant to with them. Ironically, the prose is wooden too:

Position the tail component in the... cutting with the dovetail saw easier... careful not to go beyond the shoulder line... repeat... set the component in the vice horizontally... corner waste... coping saw will remove most of the waste... pare out with a chisel... work from both sides... finish to the shoulder line.

When Jesús found such a book on my bench, he threw it the length of the workshop straight into a bin. I was taken aback both by the extraordinary accuracy of the throw and his disgust. "Nonsense," he said, "that's like a doctor having a family health encyclopaedia."

Most woodwork magazines were similar. The magazine cover usually showed a man – usually one of the few staff the magazine boasted – with a tool in his hand, looking as if he were about to do something wonderful. The pieces on which he worked were characterless. It wasn't the world as I knew it and the workshop which surrounded him was sterile.

Between the covers were straightforward projects with simple plans an enthusiast would feel proud to complete. Sometimes there would be a profile of an individual with a gallery of his work. This was better, but they were producing work for middle class people who thought they were helping the local tradesman. There were also reviews of the latest power tools and workshop machines. Manufacturers relied on the magazines to promote their products, so were keen for magazines to feature them. There was nothing in the pages for me.

The magazines closest to my skills promoted design above everything else so that the execution of the design was poor. When it *was* respectable, it was machined. If it were a dovetail, it was horrible.

There would be features on furniture-making courses accompanied by galleries of students' work. All I could do was pity them. If they had had a feeling for wood before they started the course, they would have it trained out of them. Then I realised that the people who enrolled on these courses were impressed by this work, which made them apply for the course in the first place.

The best way to learn is to sweep the workshop floor while a craftsman works. When he is accustomed to your presence, he will begin talking to you. Eventually, if you are fortunate, he will show you how to do what he does. Your learning, though, begins the moment you take the brush in hand. The floor will have dust from saws, shavings from planes, chips from mortise chisels. You recognise what tools do to wood, recognise the characteristics of different species from their waste. All this before you get to do these things yourself. You've nearly given up wanting a tool in your hand when the craftsman asks you to pass him a hammer. This is how he acquired *his* skills.

It takes years before you can think, *Yes, now I can make what I'd like to make. I have the skills.*

Two craftsmen will be able to make the same piece but you will be able to tell the difference between them. Two designers will be given the same brief but will produce different answers. A great craftsman combines craft and design to create his signature.

I loved the high-beamed air of the workshop and the natural light the glass roof let in above my bench, lit like an altar. There was something extraordinary about this scene: the moments that lay ahead of me throughout the day, the universe of each moment with a tool in hand, a planet of design, a moon of decision. I got carried away with such thoughts at times, overwhelmed by what I had given myself to, tears running down my cheeks. These ecstasies were so powerful as to stop me from being able to work for the rest of the day. I would have to recover from it as one's body recovers from an orgasm.

That was when I realised I would have to go back to Wales on a permanent basis. Accessing Napper was far more difficult than tracking down the others. I had not really considered this, but of course it seemed completely in keeping with his personal trajectory that he should be the centre of attention in some way. It suited him. Although I tracked him down easily enough to his home, there was no one place around which I could design a meeting between him and my darling. I needed a permanent base to which I could bring him.

There was no rush.

So I bought the smallholding below the cattle grid at Twmbarlwm overlooking Pant-yr-eos[141] Reservoir. I didn't need to concern myself with the house because I would live as simply as I had done in Spain, but the workshop had to be just so and the room in which I would finally achieve my life's purpose would be a studio of light.

I enjoyed the drawings and specifications for the building work. By this time, of course, my darling was complete, but as much as she pleased me I continued to be open to possibilities when they suggested enhancing her aesthetic or practicable presence.[142]

---

[141] Hollow of the Nightingale

[142] I think it was W.H. Auden who said that a poem is never finished, merely abandoned. This was my attitude to my angel. She was going to fulfil the task I had set myself so many years before and deserved that attention. Auden's poem "Musée des Beaux Arts" describes Pieter Brueghel's *Landscape with the Fall of Icarus* beautifully (about 1558, Musees des Beaux-Arts de Belgique, Brussels). However, I was more interested in the wooden plough than Icarus when *I* saw it

SPANISH FLEW

In the latest of our master craftsman series, editor Bob Harris travels to Spain to meet the great Sebastian Del Arbol.

I was filled with excitement at the prospect of meeting Del Arbol and I wasn't disappointed. Trained by the legendary Jesús-María Barriales, who died so tragically, his work has a reputation for extraordinary craftsmanship and equally extraordinary design. So I was delighted when he agreed to my visit after so many requests have been turned down previously.

Del Arbol is a quiet man but his work is not: its quality shouts! "I only accept what excites me," said Del Arbol. "It has to affect me in some way, then I sketch some features and begin to design. The design and craft are inseparable."

STUDIO
He granted me access to a personal project which he keeps in a studio, a room lit brilliantly with spots to examine – or in this case, appreciate – the work. The moment the lights flashed on took my breath away. I never thought I would ever see something so magnificent. In essence it was a chair, which is like saying a painting by Picasso is a picture.

SIGNATURE
The brief which Del Arbol set himself was to make a piece which combined his three personal 'signatures': outstanding craftsmanship, fulfilment of purpose and what he calls 'surprise'. No craftsman would argue with the first two but

I had to press him on 'surprise'.

"It's about the design, what will set it apart. It is something which causes a sharp intake of breath."

In fact, every component made my heart skip a beat. The scrolled arms, fantastically carved wings (yes, wings), the dovetails. And what's more, all of it is hand-made. There is no machinery in the workshop at all.

PHILOSOPHY

"It's essential to have a relationship with the wood you are working with," said Arbol. "When you use a machine you are divorcing yourself from the nature of making. The craftsman and the timber make together and machinery gets in the way of expressing that relationship."

When I pointed out that dovetail jigs would create perfect joints and save time he was not surprised. "Yes, they create machine-made perfect, which is quite different from hand-made perfect. I have a different relationship with every joint I cut.

"Were I to see one of my pieces again I would relive the joints and shapes I had made. If I were to use a machine I would make pieces which were empty. In my opinion, it's not bespoke unless made by hand completely."

CHEEK

By this time I was desperate to sit on the chair in front of me, which looked like a cross between a throne and a work of art. But the answer was no.

"It's not complete," said Del Arbol. "Not even I have tried it."

One thing was for certain, whoever sat on it

first was going to experience the most beautiful piece I have seen. Ever.

I didn't think it was possible for Elena to get any more beautiful but she did. Each time I saw her I would be struck by it. I took it as a good sign. After all, she was going to be mine. We would be together. I would be a father to her children and we would touch each other like the two spheres of the Love Spoon I had given her, cut from the same piece of timber, part of the same grain. The love would be pure because there would be no 'drive' from me that could sully how I expressed it.

I wondered what it was that caused her to look more beautiful each time I saw her and realised why it appeared true to me. It was her 'surprise'. Somehow each of her features managed to draw attention to itself – her ear for instance, with her hair hooked behind it. Why was it that I would notice this at a particular time? 'Surprise'. There was something within her which made some part of her beautiful at a specific moment so there was always a 'surprise' for me when I saw her. An eye. The shape of a finger. The hollow between her nose and eye.

I needed to include some aspect of Elena in my darling. But what? It annoyed me to some extent that I was identifying the need for more changes. I was determined, having come this far, to make the most magnificent piece and it had to be right. If it meant a last-minute change for the integrity of its design and purpose, then so be it. That Elena should be part of that seemed only natural somehow. A surprise for a surprise.

It was impossible to capture the feature I might have been considering with a profile gauge. Even if I ever found her asleep, the gauge would require too much pressure to copy what it was pressed against. I suppose I could have drawn her but I would have to disguise why I was drawing the particular feature, creating neither a decent drawing nor an accurate representation. It troubled me for a great deal of time and seeing her as I pondered this merely intensified the need I had identified. I was looking at an *Athene noctua* when it came to me. It was the feeling I had when I saw its huge eyes in its head. I would try to represent in wood one of the *feelings* I had when I saw Elena. This was so unusual for me, abstract rather than concrete.

I made some sketches of organic forms but all unsatisfactory because I was working with a memory of Elena. I needed to work in the intensity of the emotion when I saw her or immediately thereafter.

"I saw you looking at my mouth," Elena said. "Do you want to kiss me?"

It was so unexpected. Yes, I had been looking at her mouth. It was so perfect and to have kissed it would in some ways have spoiled it.

"You *were* looking, weren't you?"

"Yes."

"Well. Do you?"

"Yes."

"Come on then."

I was confused. I had been worshipping her from afar for as long as I could remember. I can't remember when I had first seen her exactly but it felt as though I had spent every second up to the fateful day wondering what it *would* feel like for my lips to touch hers. The electricity through me again, at last. My lips touched hers and I could taste tobacco which at once disgusted and excited me, like the bitterness of coffee when you haven't had it for a long time. I didn't know she smoked. The surprise. It made me want to kiss her and kiss her and kiss her.

She is not for you.

Again I was confused.

Mon amie.

Oh no.

It is not real.

I was kissing Elena.

Wake up.

The bastard.

This will not do.

I opened my eyes to see him leaning against my chest of drawers.

"Thanks."

For what, monsieur?

"For nothing."

He banged his cane on the floor. **There is no reward for being wicked.**

"There is for me."

Your reward will be everlasting.

"It's what I have been tuned to all my life. Ecstasy."

But what follows?

"I shall be with Elena."

No, no, no, monsieur. You will serve my cousin for ever.

"I think I shall tie you to a tree and shoot you with a hundred arrows."

His eyes opened wide and he disappeared. I was left with the taste of the kiss of tobacco and tried to remember whether Elena did smoke now or as a teenager. I was sure I would have remembered.

Robert Thompson[143] made his furniture famous by carving a mouse on his pieces. It became his trademark. Immediately after seeing Elena I felt as if I had been lit up, like a bulb in whose vacuum Elena was my filament, zinging. I studied the inside of a clear bulb, those ultra-thin pieces of metal coiled together with something as fine as one of the hairs on her head. I drew a motif that I would simplify in order to carve it into one of the arms of my darling. Oh, what a strawberry moment it was to see it carved, to see her complete, to see her ready!

[143] The Mouseman of Kilburn, Yorkshire (1876–1955). Maker of Arts and Crafts furniture

Chapter Twenty-three

The Severn Bridge is closed to high-sided vehicles because of the winds and when I pass the anemometer it is spinning furiously. David Niven sits in full flying gear next to me, talking to base on the radio. He says he's going to jump without a parachute. I'm going to stay with the van. The road is raised so high that I'm looking over the railings on each side. What a design fault: not to have built sides to protect vehicles from the wind whipping up the estuary and whirring around the towers from which the road is suspended. As heavy as the van feels, the wind hits the sides as if it's trying to push it this way and that. The van lurches across the road as I pass the first tower and I think for a moment that my darling and I will end up embracing in the filthy depths of the river below.

I manage to keep control and glance at Niven looking out the window which he has opened. He's talking into the radio. The next tower is coming up and I'm aware that I'm gripping the steering wheel too tightly. Then there's a bang as the door slams and I see Niven flapping over the railings into the grey sky, changing into a Herring Gull and tumbling out of sight.

I am two thirds of the way across the bridge now and everyone is driving carefully, leaving a good gap to the vehicle in front. *She's safe in the back, she's safe in the back*, I keep telling myself.

You're not a very good driver if your passenger has to jump out.

"I think you should meet my darling."

I know all about your 'darling'.

"So why not meet her? She's very lovely."

Oui, oui, she is. But you use her badly.

"I give her life."

No monsieur, what she kills gives her life.

"But it's me who has made her."

You are a shaper not a maker.

"I make great things."

We are getting nowhere, *mon amie*, and you

141

will have to come with me soon. My cousin is, how you say, not nice.

The gull with Niven's head sweeps up and over the bridge making its terrible noise in front of the van. I stand on the brakes and skid on to the hard shoulder as everything in the back shifts. The Conductor is gone.

There is only one maker, comes through the radio.

Everything behind me has moved but she is fine wrapped in the blankets.

At first I think the door is stuck but it is the wind pressing against it. When I do get out the door slams back. I should have got out the passenger side but that would have been into the traffic. The wind whips the water towards me like a ploughed brown field. The light moves upon it like mercury.

There is a ghostly sound which grows and dies, grows and dies. I look around for the Conductor until I realise it's the wind whistling through a mortise in each lamppost. I step over the barrier, down onto the footpath and look over the railing which trembles in my hands as the traffic passes. Nothing.

On the horizon I can make out Twmbarlwm.

I saw her coming up the lane and she waved when she saw me, then ran from the gate and threw her arms about me. "Welcome home!"

I hugged her tightly.

"Yes," I said, "I suppose you're right."

Her cheek was hard against mine and she was pressing into me. I could feel her breasts and hips against me. She turned around and looked out over the view.

"I never used to give this place a second look," she said.

"I love it." As soon as I said that I became self-conscious. Love it? Yes. I did. It was the perfect spot, just below Twmbarlwm, surrounded by birds and close to Napper and Elena. And at this instant she was here. As she turned to look at the view she kept an arm around me and I around her. Her hand slipped into mine and something went right through me.

"You going to show me around?" she said.

"I've only just got here. I haven't been able to do much."

"You can tell me what you're *going* to do." She smiled and flashed her eyebrows. "There's so much space."

"The most important thing is the workshop."

"What about the house?"

"I need to get the workshop up and running first."

"I want to see the house."

So I took her into the kitchen. There was the table onto which Jesús had put the coffee cups that first day at Casa Arbol.

"Mmm. See what you mean about just arriving. There's a fair bit to do here." She was looking around the walls at the paintwork.

"It's fine for me," I said.

She was in *my* kitchen. Stacey had been in the same space as me but this was so very different. I watched Elena as she inspected the cupboards and made little comments to herself. "You've got mice droppings in this one."

"Ah well, to be expected."

"Tell you what, you get the workshop up and running and I'll come and do some stuff in the house."

Elena's surprise. Again. She was beautiful outside and beautiful inside. I didn't know what to say.

"Well…"

"Go on, I'm offering."

I was thinking about what she would do to my house, though I hoped it would be *ours* sometime. I tried to think. Images of her house rushed through my mind: oh no, I couldn't have that aesthetic here.

"You say what you want and I'll do it."

I hadn't considered the house at all and here I was determining its future – our future – on the spot. "I'll think about it."

"Suit yourself."

"No, no, I shall. Thank you."

The house would illustrate and blend our differences. In time I could show her and gradually create a house like Webb's, internally at least, Elena and me completing the work as we moved about it.

Sitta europaea,[144] *Athene noctua, Buteo buteo, Aythya fuligula*[145] and *Aythya ferina*[146] were the birds of note at Pant-yr-eos.[147] Rhododendron blistered the far bank in the summer and *Sylvia atricapilla* thrilled the branches in Craig-y-Merchant, the deciduous wood overlooking the water. I would do a once-round of the reservoir then walk up through the small valley through which the stream ran to the water. I would sit here and watch the trees grow.

I saw Napper from a distance with two boys who looked just like him. They were coming up to the age we had been when he had ruined me. I wondered whether they were doing similar things to what their father had done at their age in this place – other boys wanting to please them as they bullied their way round school, spoiling the lives of others and being attractive to girls. Napper nodded and smiled when he saw me.

"This is a very good friend of mine from way back," he said to his boys. He held out his hand and we shook hands. Then I did the same with the boys. "Jonathan and Christopher," he said, "this is Sebastian."

"Oh yeah, you're the furniture man," said Christopher.

"That's right," I said. I was pleased Napper had spoken about me to his boys.

"Nothing to do with me," Napper said.

"Mam goes on about you," Christopher explained.

I didn't understand. "I know your mum?"

"She's talked about you a lot. You've been to ours to pick her up," Jonathan said. "You gave her the spoon thing."

"Elena's your mum?"

"Yes."

"Spoon?" Napper said flatly.

"I gave her a Love Spoon, you know. Just a token after such a

---

[144] Nuthatch
[145] Tufted Duck
[146] Pochard
[147] And despite its Welsh name, I had *never* seen a Nightingale there

long time not seeing her." I became pathetic in front of him again, self-conscious and weak.

"A Love Spoon," he said.

"Yeah." I could have been tied to the tree again, waiting for the next impact.

"You should see it, Dad. It's brill," said Christopher.

Two blows in one. My stunning little carving reduced to a curtailed adjective by a teenage boy who was Napper's.

I was aware of the embarrassment I was experiencing but Napper appeared not to sense it. "That's such a thoughtful gift, to have made something like that."

"Well, you know, it's nothing to me, making things all the time. Just knocked it up in an hour or so. People like that kind of thing, don't they?" Now I was sounding like Dog or Bull or Ev.

"Indeed they do."

Indeed they do! Where did he get that from? The boy who had destroyed me had actually had two boys – my boys – with Elena and now used such expressions as *indeed they do*. But why didn't I know about all this? Why didn't I know that she'd married Napper? Why didn't she ever tell me?

"I thought you knew," she said easily when I took her up on her offer to help me. We were sitting at the kitchen table with Jesús's coffee cups between our hands.

"No," I said. "I had no idea. You never mentioned it."

"Well I knew how much you disliked him and his friends and didn't want to spoil our time together."

That hit me. "Our time together?"

"Yes. There would've been bad air hanging between us."

I hadn't heard that expression either – *bad air* – but I knew what she meant.

"Yes."

"Am I right?"

"I suppose so." I concentrated on my coffee for a while. "Do you like our time together?"

She took her hand from around her coffee cup and placed it on my arm from where its heat travelled up to my shoulder and neck and into my head. "I love our time together."

Surprise. Elena's.

"I do, too." I looked into her face and felt odd. "I like you being here very much."

"I'm glad. I couldn't believe it when you said you were coming back."

"I love this," I said, "you there and me here. It feels right."

"I know what you mean."

"Do you?"

"Yes. But these things are, well… I want to be careful after Matt and stuff."

"The boys look just like him."

"Don't they!"

"They are handsome."

"Yes."

"Do you think they'd like me?"

"This isn't about them."

"You once said to me that I could still be a father."

"Well, you can. But this is about you and me."

"But I can't give you what you need."

"You don't know what I need."

I didn't know what to say. She was right, of course. But I just took it as read that she would want physical as well as emotional love. It was like a mortise with a tenon that didn't fit. "What about sex?"

"One thing I've learned," she said, "is that love is far more than sex."

I tried to understand what, if anything, she was implying about Napper by that. "I can't have sex," I said.

"No, you can't have *intercourse*. Sex is more than just intercourse, too."

As much as I tried to search for some drawer from which I could pull something to say, I remained dumb. I got up from the table and looked out of the window as if there might be something there.

"I wanted the boys to be my boys," I said.

"When you saw them, you mean?"

"No. I've always wanted you, ever since we were in school."

"I know you liked me, the way you were with me. But things were different. I was different."

"I used to talk to you just to hear your voice."

She laughed.

"I did."

"Well you'll be hearing it a lot more, if you want."

"That would be lovely." Be lovely? The words hung around to acknowledge that it was I who had uttered them. I was telling Elena what I felt. It was what I had been longing for my whole life. And here we were in a place which would be our home, about to begin our life together. I only had to kill Napper. "What about Napper?"

"What *about* Napper?"

"He's their father, their real father."

"Yes. But there's nothing between us."

"Didn't look like that when I bumped into him at your house."

"What do you mean?"

"You said you'd do anything for him."

"Years ago I would have. It's not like that now." She came and stood next to me. "Just look at that."

In front of us were the yard and the barn and the future.

"You going to help me here, then?"

"That's what I said."

"Nothing fancy, just quality, that's all I want."

"Whatever you want."

I remembered Stacey naked and asleep on her side in a square of light on the bed. The sun did not touch her face so I could look at her for some time before leaving the room again. She was the most beautiful design I had seen up to that point yet there was an absence within her for which Bull, Dog, Ev and Napper were responsible. It had made me look forward to when everyone was out of the way and Elena could be appreciated as she was meant to be.

I was on the barn roof fixing it up for the workshop. The roof had been replaced at some point with corrugated sheets bolted to the grand arrangement of rafters and trusses. The roof structure itself was wonderful but I needed to replace the sheeting with glass as far as possible. Elena appeared in what was going to be the workshop below and called up. "How you doing?"

"Good. It's a great space. And the light is superb. Much better than I expected."

"That's a nice surprise."

I nodded and smiled and enjoyed looking down at her from that height.

She held up a cup. "Coffee?"

I went down to her and we sat on the low wall outside the barn.

"How do you feel about Matt coming round, you know, with the boys?" I was glad I thought twice before speaking because my first reaction was to utter something vile about not wanting him within a mile of my space and Elena. But then I realised it could be just what was necessary: I would not have to design the visits – Elena would be doing it for me. It removed a significant element of fulfilling my goal. I could not believe my luck. "I know I'm biased," Elena went on, "but it's been a long time, and it would be nice for us all to be together."

"Would it?"

"Yes. I want the boys to get used to you, and if their dad's with them, you know, there's like continuity."

"I see." I couldn't, really. I was just thinking of having Napper there, getting him comfortable with being there. Killing him.

"Don't you think?"

"Yes. I suppose."

Elena took the empty cup from me and walked across the yard. I went back to the roof. I could see her in the kitchen window and she smiled and waved. I don't know why I had thought our relationship could have been anything other than this easy comfort, where we were happy merely to be near each other. And soon there would be just us and the boys with nothing at all to mar the surface of our relationship.

I could have brought the nest boxes with me but to have introduced nest sites in Spain then removed them would have been mean. So I had left them in situ and hoped they would serve the birds for some time to come. It meant that I had to start again and in doing so I would benefit the local birds and keep my hand in. It would be good to encourage *Sitta europaea*, *Dendrocopus major*[148] and *Athene noctua* I had seen around the house. I also thought I could put up something special for the *Delichon urbica*[149] and *Hirundo rustica*.[150]

When I heard the car pull in I stopped what I was doing and went out to find them looking around the yard. Elena kissed my cheek. The boys shook my hand and Napper surveyed the place from where he stood until I approached him, when he took my hand strongly.

"Long time since I was up this way. Looks as if you've been busy," he said, looking over to the barn.

"That's the workshop," I said, "would you like to see?"

Elena butted in. "Plenty of time for that," she said. "Have a wander, boys. Come on you two," she ordered. "Let's go in." Napper and I followed her.

"Are you busy?" said Napper.

"I'm always busy."

"I was wondering if you could make something for me."

"Gosh." The word hung in the air. I realised I actually said it or thought it quite often. I had not said it when I lived here as a boy. I could not recall Jesús ever saying it either and wondered where I had picked it up. "Yes, I'd like to. Always got time for a friend." I was getting worse. First *gosh*, now *friend*, though the latter felt foreign in my mouth because I did not talk about having friends. "What were you thinking of?"

"A piece of furniture."

"You know it would be expensive?"

"Yes."

"No, I mean very expensive."

Napper considered this. "Well, if it's too expensive I'll tell you but I'd still like something."

---

[148] Great Spotted Woodpecker
[149] House Martin
[150] Swallow

"Okay." I wondered what he could possibly want. I certainly knew what was suitable for him and it was waiting for him, and my limbs ached as if I were my darling waiting to flex hers. "You can have what you want, really."

"I was thinking of something straightforward like a table or chair."

"Well the first thing I need to tell you is that nothing is straightforward. Whatever I make will go through the same process. Each piece I make is unique and each component of that piece is unique, so the demands upon me are similar each time. That's why everything is so expensive."

"By straightforward I meant something I can use every day."

"That's good. The pieces I make are meant to be used. If it's a table or chair then you'll get a great deal of use out of it. Be great if you could have a table and a chair but perhaps money will constrain you. Generally speaking, the chair would cost less. It depends on how elaborate it is."

"Let's go for a chair, then."

"You should have a think about it rather than trying to decide on the spot. Think about what you will use it for, where and when, that kind of thing, then I can do some sketches and you can tell me what you think."

"That sounds good."

"Very good," Elena said. "Wish I could afford something amazing."

"You got a Love Spoon," Napper said.

"Yes, but a piece of furniture, I mean, wow!"

"I'm sure we can sort something out for you, too," Napper said.

"One at a time," I said, which sounded as if I were telling two children to stop talking over each other as well as meaning only one project at a time.

Elena looked at me. "Maybe. Shall we show Matt around?"

I told *Furniture* that I would only contribute if I could write about whatever I wished. They agreed. I imagined all those Sunday carpenters with expensive kit who were expecting one of my designs they could make for themselves. That I should write about making bird boxes caused me to chuckle. It didn't matter if they were fine pieces or not – they were making homes for birds! **... and in making a nest box – or what I prefer to call a bird box – the craftsman can carry out the essential aspects of any project with which he is presented: design, drawing to scale and making the individual components for the specific whole... some of the boxes I make become so elaborate that I would not be surprised to see them in estate agents' windows!**

Small boxes with holes	Blue Tit, Coal Tit, Great Tit, Marsh Tit, Willow Tit, House Sparrow, Tree Sparrow, Nuthatch, Pied Flycatcher, Redstart
Large boxes with holes	Great Spotted Woodpecker, Little Owl, Starling
Open-fronted boxes	Blackbird, Robin, Pied Wagtail, Spotted Flycatcher
Very large boxes	Barn Owl, Tawny Owl, Kestrel, Stock Dove, Jackdaw

The illustration shows the basic one-plank box, so called because you only have to cut it to size and drill a hole. Easy. But with a little thought you can turn a butt-jointed box into a showcase of your skills... use dovetail joints to denote how seriously you take all your work. Hey, you could use *all* the dovetail joints! Every craftsman needs to practise, so why not kill two birds with one stone?

Chuckle indeed.

Chapter Twenty-four

"I don't remember you doing Woodwork," Napper said.

"I didn't take it. Wasn't really inspired by tea trays, teapot stands and football rattles," I said.

"They did more than that at 'O' Level, I think."

"What about you two?" I said to the boys.

"It's CDT[151] now," Christopher said.

"Do you like it?"

"Teacher's crap."

"Yeah," added Jonathan, "and we hardly ever get to make *anything*."

"Well you're welcome to make what you want here. I've got everything you need."

"Great!" said Christopher.

"When the workshop's finished."

"Thanks," Napper said.

"It'll be good. I can show them some things."

"You're very lucky, you two. Sebastian's work is famous."

"'Famous'?" I said.

"It is."

"Stop it Matt," Elena said, "you're embarrassing him."

"Is it, Dad?" Jonathan said.

"Yes. You got something you can show them?" Napper said.

"You saw the spoon, didn't you," I said.

"You got something else? Something more substantial?"

All my work is substantial. Everything I've ever done is made with the same attention to design and skills. Size and purpose don't determine it as substantial or otherwise. "I'll see what I can find." It is a truth that craftsmen do not actually have much of their own work in their home. But there were a few things I had made for which I had determined a need. I left the room and returned with something I put into Christopher's hands.

[151] Craft, Design and Technology

"What is it?" he said.

I stood marvelling at the craftsmanship being inspected by Christopher and Jonathan and Napper. Elena looked at me and smiled.

"It's a bird box," I said.

"Doesn't look like one," Napper said.

He was right. I had used a variety of hardwoods to make what was ostensibly a Georgian house, complete with a grand portico, fan-lighted door and a sash window through which to see in.

"It's incredible," Napper said, turning it round in his hands.

"Quite elaborate." I held out my hands to take it. "I even made the roof as a Georgian roof might have been built." I turned it over to show them the beams and rafters.

"Wow!" Jonathan said.

We were all standing in the middle of the room passing the box from hand to hand.

"It's not a piece of furniture, though, is it?" said Napper.

"No, it's a house," Elena replied.

"So it is," he said. "A house. Makes me wonder what my chair will be like."

"I'll give you some books to take away which might help you decide what you want."

"That'd be good."

When it was time for them to go, Elena stood next to me as the others got in the car.

"Aren't you going with them?"

"Thought I'd hang around here for a while, if you don't mind."

"Course not."

The boys waved from the windows as they pulled out of the yard and Napper beeped several times as they went down the lane.

In the more naïve paintings of Saint Sebastian he is often depicted as a pin cushion. Benozzo Gozzoli's fresco[152] in San Gimignano shows him stiff with the model's pose, reed pen in right hand,

---

[152] *St Sebastian* (on the pillar) (1464–65). Absidal Chapel, Sant Agostino

arrow in left and over twenty arrows in his torso. His head is inanimate, as if Gozzoli has threatened to shoot him for real if he moves a muscle, so he glances to his left to see what is going on behind the painter.

"What birds would you like to make your boxes for?"

"What's the choice?" Christopher replied.

"Well, around here there are robins, blackbirds, tits, starlings and larger birds that would use a box like jackdaws and woodpeckers or owls. But I think you ought to make something for the little ones."

"Let's do that then," Christopher said, "right Jon?"

"Yep."

"The tits like a complete box with a hole as an entrance but robins and blackbirds prefer an open front."

"I like blackbirds. I'll do that one," Jonathan said.

"Okay, I'll go for the hole one."

"Good. Here's the timber."

"Funny looking wood," Jonathan said.

"It's a mixture of off-cuts. This is *Swietenia macrophylla*, otherwise known as Brazilian mahogany, this is *Ulmus procera*, otherwise known as elm and this is *Fagus sylvatica*. That's beech to you."

"Cool," said Christopher.

Again, an empty adjective, one I didn't expect to hear, to encapsulate three species with which I had endeavoured to create wonderful pieces of craftsmanship.

"Yes, they can be. These are going to be lucky birds, but we're only nailing and screwing the pieces because they're going to be out in all weathers. Here's a drawing for you." I showed them a basic drawing which showed them the measurements for cutting the back, sides, front, roof and base. "You can do everything the same apart from the front. I've already pencilled each piece to identify which component it should be. All you have to do is cut it to size. Because it's so simple, you'll only be using the saws and hammers."

"What about looking inside?" Christopher said.

"That's easy for the open fronted one but you would have to

hinge the top for the tit box, and I don't think it's a good idea. Any disturbance is too much disturbance as far as I'm concerned."

Christopher pulled a face.

"C'mon Chris," Jonathan warned.

"Okay, okay, sorry. When will the birds use them?"

"There's nothing to say they will. We make them and put them up where we've seen the birds we're making them for and hope for the best. They're not just for nesting either, they might be used for roosting, too."

"Cool."

"Mmm, cool," I repeated.

"It is good, though," Jonathan said, "it's like making your own home."

"It's not for you, arsehole," mocked Christopher.

"I know!" Jonathan cuffed Christopher and they squared up to each other.

"The birds are waiting," I said.

They pulled faces at each other and backed off. "Right, take a side of the bench each. I've put out the tools you are going to need. You will have to cut each piece to size first."

"Right, I'll let you get on with it, shall I?" I stood back and took in what I was seeing. The boys were in the workshop. This was the life, the new life to which I had committed myself. The workshop was stunning, a most beautiful space. The light from the glass roof was superb and everything in front of me seemed to be shining. Then I watched the boys. Was that how I had been when I first went to Jesús? Even watching them trying to mark out the timber for cutting was a shock. The differences between them became apparent quickly: Christopher rushed and Jonathan considered. But they both struggled with the tools. When they had marked each piece for size, they had to use a rip saw which wobbled in their hands.

"I can't keep to the line," said Christopher.

"Bloody thing, nor me," replied Jonathan.

It took me back to my first attempts with Jesús.

"This saw's massive," Jonathan continued. "Feels like trying to cut with an aeroplane wing."

That brought a smile to my face. "Don't worry, accuracy isn't paramount for these. I'll tidy it up if it needs it." I was teaching my boys in my workshop.

Once they had finished cutting down the grain they used panel saws to cut the pieces to length across the grain. The sides had a square bottom and sloping top to accommodate the fall of the roof. The sound of cutting across the grain with a finer-toothed saw was quite crisp, whereas the rip saw sounded as if it were chewing its way through the wood.

I was feeling what it was like to hold the tools for the first time, the strange balance of the combination square, the tips of the saws so far away from the hand they could have been fishing rods, the heft of the hammer.

"We'll screw the front on, Christopher, so we can remove it to clean the box out at the end of the season. You can do the same if you want, Jonathan, but it's not really necessary, being open. It'll mean you can use the hand drill, though. Do you want to cut the hole yourself, Christopher?"

"Yep!" he said.

"We'll do it the hard way," I joked, "using a drill and coping saw."

Jonathan and I watched Christopher compass a one-inch circle on the front piece. I gave him a hand drill with a bit large enough to pass a coping saw blade through. He drilled the hole and I set up the saw for him. "Let me start you off. You need to put the piece as low as you can in the vice so it's as solid as can be, then we saw. If you thought the rip saw was difficult, wait till you've had a go at this. The coping saw blade cuts on the back stroke."

I cut a quarter of the way round then Christopher took over.

"Oh no," he said, "you made it look easy!"

Jonathan laughed. "Give me a go."

Christopher let him. He was better but still the hole needed tidying, which I did with a gouge on a bench hook.

"We'll use these to nail the components together," I said, showing them a panel pin. Oval-wired nails are a little too vigorous for our purposes. These will be a little more delicate." I showed them how to hold a piece in the vice and support the other piece while nailing. "Here, Christopher, hold them like this and I'll show you how to use the hammer."

"It's only a hammer and a nail. I'm fine."

So I gave him the hammer. He held the pin between the finger and thumb of his left hand and struck with the hammer. "Shit!" he said as the pin bent over.

"Serves you right, cocky sod," Jonathan said.

"Would you like me to show you now?"

"Go on, then."

"Let the hammer do the work. By the time the head strikes the pin there's a huge amount of force concentrated on that one spot. Hold the hammer like this and move your wrist not your arm. It controls the swing and presents the head squarely." I knocked in two pins cleanly. "Now you."

This time he took it much more carefully. He smiled to himself when the pin went in without bending.

"Fantastic!" Elena said.

"Mam, how long've you been there?" Jonathan moaned.

"Ages."

"You could've helped," Christopher said.

"They're your boxes not mine."

"What do you reckon?" said Jonathan holding up his work so far.

"Not as easy as it looks," Christopher asserted.

"Sebastian makes it *look* easy," said Jonathan.

"You're doing a great job. It's practice that's all, lots and lots of practice," I said. "Let's finish them and put them up, shall we?"

Though it wasn't my land on the other side of the lane, the fields sweeping down to the reservoir were not out of bounds. There was an acceptance that you could walk over neighbours' fields, then if anything untoward was discovered such as a broken fence or gate, or injured livestock were found, you could let your neighbour know. There was also a footpath down the field from the crossroads down the lane, which led to the wood overlooking the water. After putting up the boys' boxes at the house, I wanted to put more around the farm. I identified more sites on neighbours' land but I was wary of anything not within my immediate control.

I woke early one morning and went into the field over the lane and stood in the long grass as the sun came up. A Little Owl passed within feet of me and settled in the hedge to my left. I didn't have my binoculars but its eyes were clearly visible from thirty yards away. It swivelled its head to take in its new vantage point. I tried to walk up on it slowly but when I got to within fifteen yards it hopped around on the branch and swept across the next field out of sight. I saw it in the same place at the same time for the next two mornings.

Chapter Twenty-five

"It's obvious, really," Napper said. "It's got to be something which blends my music, traditional techniques and your skills."

"The latter's not a problem. But you will have to give me more clues about the other two."

"Well, I listen to music all the time, in the car, at home – can't live without it. Rock, mostly."

"Right."

"And I really liked the stick chairs in the books."

"That's going back a bit."

"So it'll blend the old world and the new."

"Mmm, I see what you mean. So you want a design to incorporate rock music and stick-chair making? That should be interesting."

"Is that okay?"

"Yes. It's great. It's whirring around in here," I said, tapping my head.

"When do you think you'll have something for me to look at?"

"A week, ten days I should think." I had the idea within the moment of him telling me what he wanted. The image was an arrow-head electric guitar standing upright, one for the back, one for each side and the necks all tied with a double-headstocked 'neck' laminated and bent to each, the headstocks slightly scrolling in invitation to the hands to grip them in a similar manner to the cello-scrolled arms of my darling. I sketched it as soon as Napper's car was out of earshot. But the last thing I wanted was the meretricious glitter and gloss of such guitars, nor would there be pick-ups or switches or scratch plate. But oh, the shape was a gift to finesse! And the double-headstocked neck would be sublime. I had visions of it completed and on display in a design museum before I had finished the sketches. This was what I would present to Napper but I did other drawings to see how far I could go with the design, including tying the necks with guitar strings. Keeping the tension correct would have been the difficulty and figuring that out was beyond Napper's price range anyway. The arrow-head seat was going to be like an overly large saddle for a wooden bicycle, sculpted for the buttocks.

I found myself getting excited by the prospect of the work ahead, something I had not felt for some time.

Sebastian Del Arbol tunes guitars to a different music

Think of chairs, and guitars don't normally spring to mind. But that's what I was presented with when a client asked for a piece which combined an interest in rock music and traditional stick chairs. It might seem to be a clash which cannot be resolved, but rather than seeing it as mixing wine and beer, I saw it as an opportunity to make a creative cocktail.

Gloss and Glitter

If you are anything like me, your rock education never really got off the ground beyond Top of the Pops as a teenager, and then only because that's what teenagers did in those days. It was required viewing if you were going to be able to have a conversation in school the next day. And as disinterested as I was in the bands (I can't even say that word without sounding self-conscious!), I remembered the gloss and glitter of the instruments being wielded by the 'musicians'. The one that immediately came to mind was an arrow-head shape, bright red and slung impossibly low from the guitarist's neck.

However, being a connoisseur of timber rather than timbre, I was keen to create a piece which would meet the demands of the client and my own aesthetic geography, so red and glossy was never on the drawing board.

I put the drawings on the bench.

"That," Napper said emphatically, "is incredible."

The guitar shape would provide stability standing on the point of each 'barb' with one on each side and one at the back.

"It's absolutely stunning."

"So, do you want to go ahead with it?"

"Yes, very much. It's stunning."

"It won't *be* the guitars. I shall use timbers and techniques to make it very much a chair rather than four guitars bolted together. That would be merely vulgar."

"You know best."

"Classical guitars are beautiful pieces of craftsmanship but electric guitars are less so. I'll steam-bend the arm, which is a technique for making Windsor chairs."

"I'm looking forward to it."

"I'll need to get you to sit on a chair for height." I fetched Jesús's grandfather's chair. "Try this."

"Ah, a stick chair!"

"Yes, it's a good one."

"You've fixed it."

"A while ago."

"Why don't you use it?"

"I am using it now. I want you to try it for size."

"I mean in the house."

"I like it here in the workshop. It belonged to a craftsman."

Napper sat on it and it was too low. I measured the bend in his knee and cut blocks to go under each leg. He tried it again and we were both satisfied with his sitting height. "Let's have coffee."

"How you getting along with Elena?" Napper said unexpectedly.

"Oh... fine."

"She likes you."

"Does she?"

"I know her."

"Yes, you do know her." The words came back at me from the wall.

"Don't you think?"

"Haven't really thought about it."

"Really? You look as if you like having her around."

"I do."

"You *must* see it."

"I don't really notice that kind of thing."

"Well, I'm telling you. She likes you and even if it didn't work out with me, there's nothing to say it won't with you. You do *like* her?"

"Yes."

"You don't seem to be crazy about it."

"I do like her."

"The boys like you too."

"They are good boys."

"Yes, they are. Even I'm surprised by them. They loved doing those boxes."

"I think Jonathan could be good at what I do."

"Maybe. Christopher hasn't really got the patience for anything which needs the attention to detail *you* give something."

"Patience can be learned."

"You think? I'm not so sure."

"I had to learn it."

"Really?"

"I used to want to finish a project within five minutes of starting it. The rewards of patience are astonishing."

"Patience is rewarding?"

"Of course. Seeing a piece completed after each component has been perfectly made! It's what the craftsman is always striving for."

"I don't get it."

"You will. Your chair will take time and when it's ready you will know what I'm talking about."

"I don't think so. You are talking about craftsmanship, which is quite different to what I'm going to think as a customer."

"Maybe. But I think you will be more aware of what I am talking about."

"Like I said, I look forward to it. What are you going to do about Elena?"

I think I shrugged.

"She wants to be close to you."

I considered what Napper was saying to me. We each played with the coffee cups.

"Be good for you both," Napper said. "What's happening with the chair now?"

"I shall turn the sketches into scale drawings." I had already prepared some but had yet to account for the height of the seat.

"Why don't you have a phone?"

"I don't need one."

"I'll pop up in a few days then."

Timber Choice

Guitars are made by specialists when they are to be used as musical instruments. But I was making a chair, so the usual methods of construction were irrelevant. I did keep the two main components - the body and neck - however, but endeavoured to make and join them with a cabinet-making ethic.

In keeping with traditional stick-chair techniques, I wanted to use Ash for the arm that would bind the necks (fig.1). Because there would be no need for a fretboard, the necks for the sides and back could be solid. I did want a contrast of timber colours, though, from dark to light for the body to the neck to the headstock, recognizing the original influence of the guitar. So it was Tulipwood for the bodies, Brazilian Mahogany for the necks and Hickory for the headstock. I chose the latter because of its durability though there would be difficulty in making fine detail. It would not be bold enough for the hand rests, which were to be Ebony, hard-wearing and a superb contrast to the rest of the chair. It also continued the music theme because it is used for the 'black notes' on pianos and in other musical instruments.

"I've never seen drawings like these," Napper said. "They're beautiful."

"I like them, too. They look good framed. I've got one or two of Jesús's – that's who trained me – in the house."

"Yes, I saw. Thought they were yours. Can I have these when you've finished?"

"I usually keep them for my records."

"I'll pay for them."

"It's all right. You can have them."

"Thank you. They're amazing."

"I enjoy doing them. It's an odd experience because it's as if I have already constructed the chair before I actually get to do it in timber. Even at the sketching stage I am experiencing the making to some extent, but the scale drawings are so precise that I feel as if I *am* making."

"I'll take your word for it. I wouldn't' understand."

"I can get very excited doing the drawings. I even keep the pencils pin-sharp because they are as precious as any of the other tools. It's as if the paper is timber – which it was once, of course – and I am cutting everything out with the pencil."

"Amazing."

"I know this might sound strange, but I can taste what I am doing sometimes."

"I definitely don't understand. Maybe it's a creative thing."

"Maybe."

"What are these?" he said, pointing to the list: *Fraximus excelsior, Swietenia macrophylla, Carya illinoensis, dalbergia frutescens* and *Diospyros ebenum.*

"They are the timbers I shall use: Ash, Brazilian Mahogany, Hickory, Tulipwood and Ebony. I think the Ebony will make it sing." But I was thinking lemon, lime, orange and strawberry. *Diospyrus ebenum* was the surprise.

Details

The element blending quintessential vernacular chair making with the electronic music world was the arm rest, made from a single piece of steam-bent Ash, with the Ebony hand rest at each end falling gently forward for warmth and comfort in the hand (fig. 2—4). I carved each headstock into a finial rather like one might find on a Georgian railing, retaining the arrow head as far as possible, again appealing to my classical taste yet also representing the danger of the rock world (figs. 3 & 4).

"You'll have to have a fitting."

"Like a suit, you mean?"

"Exactly."

"No wonder these things are so expensive."

"That's why it's bespoke. This chair is for you and only you. It will be comfortable as well as being a wonderful object. Now that I have done the drawings I shall get on with making the model."

"Can't you just go ahead? I mean, you've done the drawings."

"The model's an opportunity to see whether the drawings actually work."

"Think I'm beginning to understand the expense, now."

"It's one thing working on paper, but were I just to go ahead with the *actual* chair and discovered a problem, *that* would be expensive. And tiresome. It would take the edge off the making experience to some extent."

"I wouldn't be able to keep my enthusiasm for so long."

"Ah, well, patience."

Napper smiled. "Yep. You certainly need that. So when do you do the model?"

"I'll get on with it straight away now that you've approved the drawings." I had already made the model and it was good. I had particularly enjoyed the making of the arrow-head bodies and the double-headstocked steam-bent arm rest.

Steaming

Because of the qualities of Ash and the nature of steam-bending, the sections are rather small. I had to be careful not to rush this process, which is the commonest error. There is a tendency to split the grain on the outside of the curve and compress it on the inside causing ripples (fig. 5). Either fault would mean having to start again. The Ebony hand rests would only be added after the steam-bending process. The contrast between the Ash and Ebony would also be enhanced by the hand rest's apparent over-sizing. Were the arm rest straight it would appear to be a double-headed arrow with oversized points.

Napper's project had occurred so naturally that I felt it was a reward for all the years I had been working towards my goal. I was sitting on the bank of the reservoir looking across at the rhododendrons reflected in the water. Each year the water waited for them to bloom to warm itself with their pinks and deep greens and it was rewarded the following year with more blooms. Such rewards were natural and augmenting.

I had gone to find the person and skills I needed to fulfil my ambitions. The acquisition of each skill had brought me closer to what was going to happen soon, and organically, it seemed to me. I had known what I was working towards but now I could barely comprehend that it was imminent. Bull, Dog and Ev had merely been stations on the way. The actual moment when I would kill Napper had been so long in my mind that I almost believed that this is where it would happen. It had felt distant when I was in Spain, like a hill on the horizon that is always there but climbed only once in a lifetime, or another country I knew existed somewhere beyond the sea's horizon. Not here. Bull, lemon; Dog, lime; Ev, orange; Napper, strawberry. And soon.

Chapter Twenty-six

"The male Wren builds several nests for the female and she chooses which one she is going to lay her eggs in," I said, as we watched a Wren busying itself low in the hedge against the lane.

"We wouldn't get very far if men had to do that," Elena said, lifting her eyebrows.

"I'd like to build a home for you," I said. She didn't reply. "Wouldn't you like that?"

There was a pause. "Why don't we build one together?"

My stomach did something odd. "I'd never have considered that."

"It's not all you," she said. "Love is two-way, half-and-half, two to tango."

"Yes, but..." I stopped to think about what it was I actually wanted to say. "Are you saying that we are a couple?"

"I thought that's where we were going."

"It's where I would like to go. But I am afraid to say."

"Okay, I'll say it: I love you," she said.

I had wanted to hear Elena say that to me since I was a boy. I had dreams in which she stood in front of me in her blue bra and said *I love you, Tim* and then kissed me perfectly with her perfect lips, keeping her eyes crushed in mine as she did so.

"I love you and think you love me," she said.

"I can't remember a time when I didn't love you."

"So there we are: we're a couple!"

"Is it that simple?"

"There's nothing complicated about love," she said, "you either love someone or you don't." She kissed me softly on the mouth.

"You kept your eyes open!"

"And...?"

"I like that."

"Good." She kissed me for longer and kept her eyes open again. Then she hugged me and pressed her face into my chest. "You have no idea what it means to have you home."

"Nor you for me to have you here," I said.

Irene's face is more or less straight-on in Georges de la Tour's *St. Sebastian Tended by Irene (à la lanterne)*.[153] There is an arrow in Sebastian's left thigh which she is holding daintily, her left hand resting on his knee. The lantern just left of centre is throwing its light onto the site on which Irene concentrates. Of the three figures, only Irene's face is lit to show her importance.

I was looking toward Pen-y-fan[154] on the horizon to the north when she put her arms around me from behind. I put my hand over hers and squeezed.

"I love you," I said. The wind took my words to the east and she did not hear me. I turned around and pressed my mouth to her ear and said it again. She took my head in her hands and pulled my ear to her mouth.

"I love you, too," and she kissed my ear, then cheek and finally mouth. The kisses felt as if they were putting down roots. She turned around to look at the view in front of us. We were facing the coast now, Flat Holm and Steep Holm adrift in the Bristol Channel's silver.[155] The clouds moved slowly about half-way up the sky if viewed as a canvas, their shadows darkening the water in large patches. Jets criss-crossed at different heights, their vapour trails showing where their little worlds had disturbed the air. And very close, a *Corvus corax* floated so near that I felt I could have touched it, and I marvelled at how perfect it was for this place, its primary feathers spread to enjoy the winds.

We came down off the tump[156] and began our way down to the house, passing the oak at the top of the tree line, a chunk bitten out of it by the wind as if it were a piece of fruit, and the soughing through the forestry competing with the jets in their high sphere. The land rippled away from us like linen-fold carving.

[153] Detroit Institute of the Arts

[154] The highest peak in the Brecon Beacons National Park

[155] Guglielmo Marconi transmitted the first wireless signals from the mainland to Flat Holm on 13th May 1897. The island is regarded as Welsh whereas Steep Holm is regarded as English. Holm is a Scandinavian word, meaning an island in an estuary

[156] That is what the locals call Twmbarlwm Mound. The very top looks like a nipple from a distance

Elena held my hand all the way down to the house and she tugged me to the fence poles opposite the yard entrance to look over the reservoir. There were men fishing, their lines just visible as they wrote each cast on the water.

"You make me feel lucky," Elena said.

"I'm the lucky one. You make me feel as if I can live again."

"Again?"

"I don't think I have lived since I was a boy."

"Since you were hurt."

"Yes."

"Of course you have. You are a craftsman. A wonderful craftsman. My craftsman. You must have lived to become what you are now."

"All yours," I said, "all yours."

"Just love me, that's all."

"You make it sound small."

"It's not a lot to ask."

"Of course it is! It's a huge thing to ask!"

She laughed. "You're teasing."

Buteo buteo floated over us and I could see its head clearly moving as it quartered the field in front of us towards the reservoir.

"We'll make this place special," she said. "This is our place, Sebastian."

The way she said my name rendered it remote, a white-sanded island swept with gentle breezes. The soft sibilance was the water washing the sand and the final unstressed syllable folded under itself like a small wave. Sometimes when she spoke my name I felt I could have been inside her.

Irene is holding the arrow so daintily in Vicente López y Portana's *Saint Sebastian Tended by Saint Irene*,[157] it looks as if she is sewing with it. Higher up the leg is a hole from which she has already removed an arrow. Sebastian's skin glows in the light I imagine is being reflected from many candles, Irene's face concentrated on the job

---

[157] (1795–1800), oil on canvas, 30 7/8" x 25 3/8", John Paul Getty Museum, Los Angeles, California

in hand. Andrea Lilo's work[158] is more delicate and precise, squared ready for scaling up and transfer. It is as important in the making of the painting as my drawings are to my work. Two figures are busy cleaning wounds, one is supporting and the candle holder looks out at the viewer with an expression which says, *Who could do such a thing?* I thought then that the Conductor had given up on me.

Working with wood every day, I had had my share of splinters from more species of timber than most people. Working on Napper's chair, a splinter of *Diospyros ebenum* punctured the palm of my right hand so that it looked like a line of thick black ink an inch long under the skin. It had snapped off so that there was nothing to hold on to. Often it is possible to merely pull out a splinter with tweezers but one such as this necessitated the use of a scalpel.

I went across to the house to find Elena who was painting the kitchen.

"Can you sort this out for me?"

"Ouch!" she said, "that's what I call a splinter."

"You'll need to slit the top layer of skin where it entered so you can get a purchase on it." I gave her the scalpel blade and tweezers.

"Let's see." She put my hand down on the kitchen table which she had pushed to the window to give her room to paint the walls. "The light's better here." She gently pushed the point of the blade against the skin and eased it open to reveal the tip of the splinter. She gripped it with the tweezers and eased it out in one. "Well, that's the biggest I've ever seen," she said, holding it up between us.

"A beauty," I said, blood oozing down my hand.

She held my hand under the cold tap and squeezed it. "I'll clean it up and you can get back to work." She put a large plaster over the wound.

"No love then?"

"You've interrupted my decorating."

"You are a callous woman. Not like Irene."

"Who's Irene?"

[158] *Figures Tending to the Wounded Saint Sebastian* (c.1596), black chalk with traces of white chalk, 10 5/8" x 9 15/16"

"She looked after Saint Sebastian when he was shot by arrows."

"Sebastian was a saint?"

"And Irene."

"I'm no saint," she said.

"You just made me better."

"I put a plaster on your hand."

"Exactly."

"Does that make *you* better?"

"Just having you here makes me better."

She smiled and pushed me out of the door. "Go on, you've taken me from my decorating for long enough as it is."

"You *are* callous."

"That's why you love me. Go. I've got a kitchen to finish."

I pretended to skulk across the yard to the workshop.

"Stop it!" she shouted.

I straightened up and went into the workshop to be greeted by Napper's guitar-chair well on its way to completion, the offending ebony on the bench where I had left it.

Chapter Twenty-seven

If you were to enter my workshop you would recognise much of Jesús's influence in the arrangement of the benches and the tools, just as Jesús's workshop took after his grandfather's. There is a continuum, a recognition of a way of doing things which changes oh-so-slightly from one generation to the next. Some of the tools may have changed in design – the hammers and saws and planes and chisels – but they did the same job fundamentally. The development of tools had made particular processes easier and, once the characteristics of the tools had been learned, it was possible to do astonishing things.

The tools in Millais's *Christ in the House of His Parents* are Victorian. They are still used today. The difference between then and now is the machinery which makes everything so much easier and quicker and cheaper. But it all gets in the way of the craftsman's communion with the grain, the wood, the earth and the sky. Hand tools allow the craftsman to *feel* at least, which circular saws, crosscut saws, planer/thicknessers, tenoners, mortisers and spindle moulders do not. To feel a species's response to the tool in your hand is to *know* it.

"I can't believe this is just the model," Napper said, standing next to the mock-up of his chair. "I'd be happy with this." Other clients had said as much when they had seen models of their commissions. "So what's all this?" he said, waving his hand at the chair in a sweeping arc.

"I've just made it from softwood species. Everything is somewhat lacking in finish. I need you to sit on it now."

Napper stood in front of it, turned, put his hands on the arm-rest and lowered himself onto the seat slowly until his whole weight was on his buttocks. Then he eased backwards until he touched the 'neck' of the back, and gripped the hand rests. "I never expected this. It's beautiful."

I stood in front of him, closed each eye in turn and looked at his position with regard to the arm each side and the length of the 'neck' rising behind him. Then I took up a position to his right and left to assess the chair in profile.

"The height of the seat is fine but I shall give you a slightly more generous seat, and raise the 'necks' for better proportion."

"You think? Feels fine to me."

"I won't be happy to let you have it in its current form."

"You will have to do more fitting then."

"No. It will be finished the next time you see it."

That night I went to see my darling. I told her that she would not have long to wait, that her moment of glory was coming soon. I looked at her and shivered and felt slightly nauseous as I saw Napper take his place and witnessed the instant of grace to which I had devoted myself.

I had not thought it would be here; I had expected it to be in Spain. My darling had changed so much since I had conceived her. What had not changed was that need for her I had experienced whilst recovering in hospital, a need that had not grown so much as expanded into a universe of desire. Napper's death would be sublime and then it would be just Irene and me.

"It's amazing," Napper said to Elena. "Just amazing."

"I know."

"You should make more for your own house," Napper said.

"No, it's always for someone else," I said.

Elena interrupted. "He's got something on the go."

I frowned at her.

"You know, your project."

"Oh, yes, that's for me. Just something for myself."

"What is it?" Napper said.

I didn't want him to know nor had I expected Elena to bring it up.

"It's a sculpture," she said.

"Oooh, let me see *that*," Napper said.

"Go on," egged Elena.

"It's not finished. Besides, it's for me."

"Oh, go on," she groaned. "We're not going to hurt it." She put on a pleading face and looked me in the eye.

"I know! I know! But it's just for me. No one's seen it. You can see it when it's finished."

"Okay then, if you feel that strongly," Napper said.

Elena poked out her tongue. "Killjoy!"

I changed the subject.

My angel. My darling. I had not tended her for some time. I need not have concerned myself because I had kept her in the same room and atmosphere in which she was going to live and love Napper. I had locked her mechanism and she was poised and patient. She looked as magnificent under the spots as Sebastian in Vicente Lopez y Portana's glowing painting. If she had been two-dimensional I would want her in an elaborate tabernacle frame. Because I had not tended her for so long I was startled when I turned on the spots. She was a bold statement of years and years of my skills and craftsmanship, her wings ready for only one more flap.

For sure, you are a wicked man, monsieur.

"I have told you again and again that I am going to do what I set out to do."

No, no, no! You can stop this. You must or you will go to my cousin. He is not nice, monsieur. He… _je ne sais quoi_. Trust me. I ignored him and walked around my angel, touching her lightly, admiring her. He blocked my way with his cane when I was about to pass in front of him. **You can carry on your work if you come with me now**, he said, drawing a circle in the air with the point of the cane.

"But my darling is ready and I am ready and he is ready. This is all I have worked for and I do not need to come with you. My achievement is here."

Come with me and you can make what you like forever.

"I have made what I like and I am not interested in forever."

And Elena?

"She will be there for me when I am done."

This is not so! He stood up sharply, pulled on each cuff and glared at me. **YOU ARE A NINCOMPOOP!**

I laughed at his expression and he disappeared instantly. He had never been there anyway.

Elena had kicked off her shoes and tucked her feet under her on the sofa. I sat next to her and she pushed herself in close to me.

"Matt loves his chair," she said. "I'm so pleased you did it."

"It's good."

"It's good to see you getting on."

I was happy that she was happy.

She took my hands in hers and squeezed. "Beautiful, beautiful hands." Then she kissed them, biting each finger gently. She kissed my mouth and her tongue explored my lips and teeth. She stood up to undress, letting her jeans fall. Her legs were fine and crisp as a Pembroke table, tapering from smooth thighs, and I was eager to appreciate their shape and texture and weight in my hands. Already I was wondering what they would feel like against my legs. O her thighs! O her knees!

She undid the buttons of her shirt and immediately I saw the healed wound from an arrow that was her navel. She was the colour of *Chloroxylon swietenia*[159] in the light of the room, the up-lighter bouncing softly from the ceiling. Her clavicles were brackets supporting her neck and head on the shelf of her shoulders. Her breasts had been filed and riffled and sanded and polished for hours and hours. They were separate and heavy as she bent towards me to slip her knickers down her legs. I was surprised to see her *mons pubis* was smooth and neat when she stood up straight again.

She took my hands to place them on her breasts. "My beautiful, beautiful hands," she said. They were cool, each the weight of a carving mallet, the nipples hard and giving as corks. Her eyes dissolved into mine as she kissed me. She undid my shirt, pushed it over my shoulders, down my arms and pulled me close to press her breasts to me. She took my hands again and kissed the fingers, stood up and put my right hand to her vagina, carved with a V-tool and veiner and skew chisel. She stroked herself with my fingers and put my middle finger inside her slowly. She showed me technique: position, rhythm. "Beautiful hands," she said quietly. She shuddered.

[159] Satinwood

Chapter Twenty-eight

My darling and I were ready. Napper would try his own chair then I would kill him beautifully.

Now that it was imminent I was calm and relaxed: everything I had *been* up to this point was for this. I *knew* it would be incredible because I had dedicated myself to becoming a craftsman and my darling was the apotheosis of my talent.

Beautifully.

When Napper arrived he was eager to see his piece and I was eager to show it to him but I had to do everything in a state of measured consideration to maintain the grace with which I wanted to kill him.

Beautifully.

The guitar chair was a triumph, of course. It was unusual for me to be held up these days by error and the project had gone smoothly. I had little feeling towards it, however, as I mostly regarded it as a fortuitous means to a fortuitous end. Now as I showed it to Napper I did concede it was a brilliant design.

"Like I said, I would've been happy with the model. This is incredible," was his first reaction. He stood back from it and walked around it and now and then he stepped forward to run his hand over some part of it. "Phew," he said, and "wow! Never thought I'd have anything like this in my house. Fantastic, isn't it?"

"I am glad you are pleased."

"Isn't it, though? Don't you think?"

"It is different for me. I have a different relationship to it as the maker."

"Believe me, this is…" He didn't finish but shook his head.

"It is always a pleasure to see the client happy."

"I'm certainly that." Finally he sat on the chair and relaxed, putting his arms on the rests, gripping the *Diospyros ebenum* arrow heads and squaring his feet on the floor. "Worth every wonderfully expensive penny."

Even in this piece the human had combined well with the craftsmanship, the 'music' of the chair expressing its perfect chord with Napper on the seat. I was right to have extended the length of the necks at the fitting, and the arrow-head motif was one of those details that made the whole project memorable and set it apart from so-so work.

Napper was mine. "Would you like to see my project?"

"What, the thing Elena was on about?"

"That's it."

"Please," he said, nodding and standing up.

I took him to the studio where my darling was waiting. I turned on the spots and there she was. Napper gasped audibly. I knew then that it was going to be easy and all I had to do was enjoy the event.

Ask a craftsman what is the most versatile tool and you will get a different answer each time.

To see Napper falling in love with my darling was a happy accident, so to speak, and would make it sweeter, if that were possible. He had been visibly moved by his commission and now he was wide-eyed in awe. As was I. My darling was majestic in the light. I had had something akin to a near-death experience, yet this was kaleidoscopic, me drawing, sharpening, cutting her components, furniture, wings and fish. They lined a tunnel at the end of which was my eye, and inside that a flight of drawers with a handwritten label on one: *Magnum Opus.*

"Unbelievable," Napper whispered. "Should be in a museum."

"You like her?" I had forgotten myself for a moment and was annoyed I had used such a personal pronoun as 'her'. I need not have worried because he was in love.

"She's amazing."

Ha! All those years. *She.* At least he did not say that she was *nice.* If he had, I think I would have killed him with a chisel.

For some it is the trusty claw hammer.

I had saved the best until last. I wished Piero and Antonio del Pollaiuolo[160] could have been there to appreciate my great work as I had theirs. Napper was the final dovetail in the project. The wings' lemon, orange, lime and strawberry feathers would flap once. If only the psychologist could have seen it. Oh the hundreds and thousands of times I had swung a hammer and shot a length of timber and cut grain! The guitar-chair had been the perfect bait. I wanted Jack Cardiff to film what was about to happen.

For others it is their combination square.

Napper walked in front of the Conductor who shook his head at me.

"So this is just for you, you said."

"That's right."

"Where does it go from here? You must have some plan for it. Use it in the house. I mean, I know it's a bit OTT but at least you'll be able to use it."

Of course it wasn't OTT for the house! It was a stupid description! "I have not thought what to do with it. I have been working on it for so long. Years in fact."

"But why?"

"It has been a joy to me. I wanted to make something extraordinary, something that showed off my skills."

"It does!"

Napper stopped to take a more concentrated look at something.

"Sit on it," I said.

"Oh no, I couldn't. It's a museum piece," he said, shaking his head firmly.

"It's fine. Go ahead. It is like all my pieces: it is meant to be used."

"No. You sit on it. I don't want to damage it."

He's a wise man.

"You are interfering," I said to the Conductor.

---

[160] The brothers who painted *The Martyrdom of Saint Sebastian* in the National Gallery, London

"Interfering?" said Napper.

It was going wrong.

It's not his time.

"*I* have decided it is time," I said.

"What?" Napper said, confused.

I went towards the Conductor and he disappeared as I got close.

"I don't understand," Napper continued. "I'm not interfering. I didn't mean to get in the way."

"I have decided, because you were so appreciative of your own chair, that you would be the ideal person to see this. Please. I want you to try it."

"All right. If it'll please you."

I was consciously trying to remember what each moment was like that I may re-live it after the event. It was going to be so *brief*. He turned around, put his hands on the rests either side of him and let his weight carefully onto the *Ulmus procera*.

The wings flapped forwards and back and bounced the spots off their feathers in a mirror-ball effect. The moment I had worked towards all my life was a sound more beautiful than the call of *Corvus corone* on a cold autumn morning, or the splash of a *Tinca tinca*[161] fighting all the way to the bank, or Elena saying *I love you*. It began with a voiceless palato-alveolar [ʃ], sped through the voiced close vowel [iː], came to a brief hiatus with the [ʃ], then back through the [iː] and stopped at the [ʃ] again. *Sheesheesh*. In. Out.

Napper died beautifully.

My darling worked perfectly.

I had an erection.

A strawberry double-plus moment.

The egg in the pan.

It was a level of craftsmanship that would only ever be witnessed by me, a moment when the piece was whole when dovetailed with its final human component. Without that it was ordinary. With it, fabulous. It was craftsmanship beyond anything Jesús could have done. Webb had been right all those years ago but not intimate enough.

---

[161] Tench

Napper had been aware of something as my darling balanced him on the fulcrum between his life and death.It was an awareness of the finest piece of craftsmanship he would witness. For me it was the joy of his joy. It was done. The cruelty uttered by that childhood event had finally been answered with measured grace. I wanted Millais to paint this masterpiece.

I took the strawberry Opal Fruit from the packet and slipped it into his pocket. "This is for you." Then I took off his trousers and pants, slit his scrotum and snipped out his testicles. "And these are for me." I went into the workshop to wash and dry them and put them in my grandfather's box with the others, which were now small and desiccated.

I went across the yard to the house to make coffee. I crossed the lane with the box and rested on the pole fence. Several gulls circled the blue water of the reservoir but too far away for me to identify which species they were. Elena came up the lane. The kiss she gave me made me feel complete.

"I thought Matt was here to collect his chair."

"He's in the studio."

She took my hand and pulled me with her across the yard.

It might even be their folding rule.

"This is your project," Elena said from the doorway. "What's it like, Matt?"

I had another erection.

"Matt?"

"He is dead," I said, without hiding my pride.

"Stop fooling around."

"He is."

She went to him and saw the mess between his legs. "What the fuck's going on! What's happened? What the fuck!" She pushed him and the wings moved as the seat registered the movement. Napper's head fell to one side. "What's happened? Stop fooling you two, I've had enough."

"My darling killed him."

"'Darling'? What do you mean?"

"This is what I have worked for ever since they tied me to a tree and took my life away."

"I don't get this. What's happened? What do you mean your 'darling'?"

"I made her to kill him, to kill *all* of them."

"*You* killed them?"

"And him," I said, nodding at Napper.

The wisest craftsman, however, will tell you that it is something you will not find in any tool box or in any catalogue.

"This is doing my head in," Elena said.

"It is okay."

"It's not okay!" she shouted. "How *can* it be okay?"

"Now we can be together and I can be a father."

"There's something wrong with you, something really fucking wrong."

I did not like to hear her using such base language. I had not accounted for Elena to witness all this but now that she had, I thought it was good. At least she would see that there would be no barriers to our life together. "It is for the best. I had to kill him. I had to kill them. It is what I have dedicated my life to achieving. And Napper was the last one. I have finished." And with that verb I felt relief, as if in saying it my mind and body could relax after so many years.

"Dedicated yourself. You *are* nuts."

"It is what I set out to do since they hurt me. I have loved you all my life and now you love me."

"Well, I've got news for you. It wasn't Napper who hurt you. It wasn't any of them. It was *me*. Me!"

I did not understand what she meant but I remained calm. She was upset, hence the base language too. "You were not there."

"I was."

"You found me."

"I came up the bank from my house and Matt gave me a spear and I threw it. They all ran and I stayed. That's why I 'found' you," she said, spitting the words out.

"Nonsense."

"I wish it was nonsense. It was me. A great shot, they said. Oh yeah, a *fucking* great shot, I think now."

I re-lived the long, long, long, long, long pause before that final blow. It *could* have been her.

"I would do anything for Matt," she said quietly.

"So you did."

"I did."

This did not happen to Saint Sebastian. And Irene had nursed him back to health. I had lost my Irene. I was vulnerable, my body and mind relaxed then eviscerated. Elena had been the heartwood of my emotional bole. She had kept things back and been untruthful. I could not love her now.

Then I had the idea for Stacey's gift, based on the tables at Café Jazz in Salamanca . It would be a table for two, the top a huge butterfly key such as those I had used to close the seat of Jesús's grandfather's chair. It was perfect because the shape presented a wide front to each person then tapered away to meet the person opposite, as if we could rest our arms on the edges and copy the angles to each other's hands in the middle. Too late.

The most versatile tool is the craftsman himself.

Elena took a packet of cigarettes from her jacket pocket and lit up expertly.

"You must not do that," I said.

"You going to give me a load of shit about how it's bad for me and how you don't want me to kill myself?"

"No. You cannot smoke in the workshop environment."

She laughed. "I should've known."

"Not to worry."

"I mean I should've known it would be nothing to do with *me*. With you, if it's wood it's in, if it's not, it's out."

I left Napper with my darling and Elena tending him.

Chapter Twenty-nine

Sebastian Del Arbol: Bob Harris Comments

It is my fervent wish that one day Sebastian del Arbol's life and work will be understood more fully and accurately than merely being the subject of hundreds of lurid headlines.

Enough has been written elsewhere about the circumstances surrounding his disappearance. It will be extremely difficult to separate the motives behind his greatest work from his standing as a craftsman, and there is no doubt that any assessment of his output from this point on will be affected by what has been learned since his loss.

But up until then he was regarded as the finest craftsman of his generation, a man who had dedicated himself to achieving that position and who could choose his commissions: an enviable position for any craftsman.

Apprenticed to the legendary Jesús-María Barriales, he underwent the strictest and most demanding training where nothing less than perfect was tolerated, and he took Barriales's hand-made bespoke philosophy to heart from the outset. When I visited his Spanish workshop for this magazine, I felt I had met someone special. I knew of his no-machinery approach and was sceptical, expecting the workshop to be equipped with a planer-thicknesser at least. But there was no machinery of any kind. Everything was done by hand, even basic sizing. His response to my incredulity was, "Who needs machines: we are the perfect example of such things."

Acknowledgements

I would like to thank Ceri Lloyd, Henry Layte, Paula Stanic, Sharath Jeevan, Antoinette Pas, Lucy Rutter, John White, Hannah Gutstein, Dominic Stevens and David Krump for their love and encouragement at the beginning; Stephen Logan for understanding the worlds we share; Ursula and Theodore for keeping my head below the clouds; Renée for more than I can express.

PERFECT ARCHITECT

"A work of stunning originality
and deftness of prose, in which
Jayne Joso explores with delicate
skill and rare empathy what
becomes of the broken hearted."
Cathi Unsworth

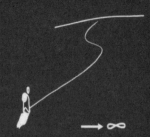

JAYNE JOSO

£8.99

"Richard Gwyn's memoir – his down-and-out vagabondage around the Mediterranean – takes us on a terrifying, funny and erudite journey through alcoholism, insomnia and liver disease to a redemptive and self-accepting wisdom. One hell of a good read."
Desmond Barry

The Vagabond's Breakfast
Richard Gwyn

£9.99

www.alcemi.eu

TALYBONT CEREDIGION CYMRU SY24 5HE
e-mail gwen@ylolfa.com
phone (01970) 832 304
fax (01970) 832 782

ALCEMI A